The Conspiracy

by

Kathi Daley

This book is a work of fiction. Names, characters, places, and incidents either are products of the author's imagination or are used fictitiously. Any resemblance to actual events or locales or persons, living or dead, is entirely coincidental.

I want to thank the very talented Jessica Fischer for the cover art.

I so appreciate Bruce Curran, who is always ready and willing to answer my cyber questions.

And, of course, thanks to the readers and bloggers in my life, who make doing what I do possible.

I also want to thank Randy Ladenheim-Gil for being an awesome editor and an even more awesome friend.

And finally I want to thank my sister Christy for always lending an ear and my husband Ken for allowing me time to write by taking care of everything else.

Books by Kathi Daley

Come for the murder,
stay for the romance.
Buy them on Amazon today.

Zoe Donovan Cozy Mystery:

Halloween Hijinks
The Trouble With Turkeys
Christmas Crazy
Cupid's Curse
Big Bunny Bump-off
Beach Blanket Barbie
Maui Madness
Derby Divas
Haunted Hamlet
Turkeys, Tuxes, and Tabbies
Christmas Cozy
Alaskan Alliance
Matrimony Meltdown
Soul Surrender
Heavenly Honeymoon
Hopscotch Homicide
Ghostly Graveyard
Santa Sleuth – *December 2015*

Paradise Lake Cozy Mystery:

Pumpkins in Paradise
Snowmen in Paradise
Bikinis in Paradise
Christmas in Paradise
Puppies in Paradise
Halloween in Paradise

Whales and Tails Cozy Mystery:

Romeow and Juliet
The Mad Catter
Grimm's Furry Tail
Much Ado About Felines
The Legend of Tabby Hollow
Cat of Christmas Past – *November 2015*

Seacliff High Mystery:

The Secret
The Curse
The Relic
The Conspiracy
The Grudge – *December 2015*

Road to Christmas Romance:

Road to Christmas Past

Chapter 1

"Tell me again why we're walking around a cemetery in the middle of the night." Mac carefully stepped over a broken headstone as a heavy fog blanketed the area, making it difficult to navigate through the scattered tombstones, wooden crosses, and barren trees that landscaped the long-forgotten cemetery.

"Because it's directly in the path between Alyson's house and the point where my car broke down." Trevor kicked a rusted beer can that someone had left behind.

"Seriously, Trev, you should think about getting a new car," Alyson Prescott commented as she wrapped her arms around herself in an effort to keep warm as a foghorn sounded in the distance.

"Sell Raquel? No way. She's been in the family longer than I have."

"You named your car Raquel?" Alyson asked.

"My grandfather did. He bought her new in 1965. She was one of the first Mustangs manufactured when Ford introduced the model in the midsixties. My granddad gave her to my dad about ten years later, and my dad gave her to me last year. Someday I hope to pass her on to Trevor Jr."

"Well, next time let's take Alyson's car," Mac suggested. "At least it's not always breaking down like yours and mine. Graveyards give me major wiggins."

"I like graveyards, especially old ones." Alyson walked over and wiped the dirt from an old headstone that was crumbling with age. "You meet the most interesting people."

"Huh?" Mac asked.

"Joseph Stillwell. A loving husband and father. He was born in 1775 and died in 1811 of cholera." Alyson pulled some weeds away from the base of the headstone and smoothed the dirt with the palm of her hand. "He's been standing here watching us."

"What?" Trevor turned his head to the right. "Where?" He turned to the left. "How?" He turned his body 360 degrees.

"Right here. You're almost standing on him."

Trevor and Mac both jumped back.

"No worries; he seems harmless enough. Joseph Stillwell, meet my friends, Trevor Johnson and Mackenzie Reynolds."

"Is he talking to you?" Mac asked.

"No. I've found that most ghosts really aren't much for chitchat. They mostly just stare at you and sort of communicate with their intent more than with words."

"So how do you know your ghost is Joseph Stillwell?" Mac asked.

"Because I saw him standing here. This is Joseph Stillwell's grave, so I put two and two together and came up with the most logical conclusion."

"What's he doing? I mean, right now? I'm not standing on him, am I?" Trevor took a step toward Mac.

"No, he's gone. I think he was surprised I could see him."

"I wonder what he wanted," Mac murmured.

"Who knows? Maybe nothing. We came to him; he didn't exactly come to us. He might just have been out enjoying the evening."

"You think?" Mac seemed doubtful.

"I don't know. Maybe. He didn't seem like he was trying to tell me anything. It's been my experience that when ghosts want something they usually come to you and sort of glare. It's like they're beckoning you with their eyes. Old Joseph, though, he just seemed to be hanging out."

Mac looked around the deserted bluff. "Do you see anyone else?"

"No. It seems pretty dead around here."

"Ha, ha. Very funny," Trevor quipped. "Seriously, though, let's get out of here before anyone else decides to show up."

"Fine with me." Alyson began walking toward the northernmost boundary of the ancient graveyard, arm in arm with her friends.

"Isn't this the land Psycorp wants to buy?" Alyson asked.

"Yeah. It's caused quite a scandal," Mac answered.

"Scandal? What scandal?" Trevor asked.

"Trevor, where have you been for the past few weeks?" Mac asked. "Under a rock?"

"Give me a break, Mac. I've been busy helping the Seacliff High Pirates win the state football championship. I haven't exactly had time to keep up with all the town gossip."

"Yeah, I guess you're right. Anyway, at last month's town council meeting the mayor reported that there's a huge budget deficit. There isn't enough money to cover even the most basic expenses for the upcoming year. We're talking major layoffs. And not just clerical personnel but police and firefighters will be heavily affected. He also reported that Psycorp, a major corporation from the East Coast, wants to establish a West Coast presence and is interested in buying the very land we're standing on. The proceeds from the sale will not only cover the deficit for next year but will also provide a surplus that can be used for the next couple of years."

"Sounds good. So what's the scandal?"

"Look around, Trev. We're standing on peoples' graves. It wouldn't be right to let them build a factory on top of them."

"Can't they move them, maybe to the cemetery on the other side of town? I mean, no one's been buried here for almost two hundred years. It's not like anyone's husband or wife is going to care. Besides, the place is really run-down. A real eyesore."

"Trev, this site was used as a burial grounds for the Native American population that first settled in this area and lived here for hundreds of years. Most of the graves aren't even marked. A few of the earliest settlers are buried here as well, which accounts for most of the headstones, but the indigenous people tended to mark graves with more perishable items that decayed long ago."

"I see your point, but do we really have an option? I mean, if the town is out of money the town is out of money. Besides, wouldn't a new factory bring jobs?" Trevor asked.

"Trevor!" Mac stopped walking. "Money to balance the budget is important, but not as important as preserving a sacred burial ground." Mac knelt down and traced the carving on a wooden headstone.

"Whoever carved this headstone obviously did so with love and care. Look at the detail, the plump little cherubs and the intricate border. *Johnny Trent, July 2, 1802–July 4, 1802. Our hearts will forever be enshrined with our littlest angel.* How sad. Someone poured their grief into this headstone. It should be left undisturbed. Little Johnny Trent deserves to rest in peace."

"Hey, guys," Alyson interrupted. "I don't mean to disrupt your lively debate, but didn't you say no one had been buried here for over a hundred years?"

"Yeah, they built the new cemetery in the early 1900s and no one has been buried here since," Mac answered. "Why?"

"'Cause it looks like we have a freshly dug grave." Alyson looked down at the pile of newly piled dirt at her feet.

"That's odd." Mac walked toward Alyson. "No one's used this cemetery for years. And there's no headstone or marker. Who do you think was buried here?"

"I don't know," Trevor joined them, "but I'm sensing foul play. And speaking of foul, what's that awful smell?"

"I have a horrible feeling it might be a corpse." Alyson grimaced. "Maybe we should call the police."

"Yeah, maybe we should," Mac agreed. "I hope it's not just a dead animal or something. It'd be embarrassing if we bothered the police because of a dead dog."

"Actually, a little doggie embarrassment would be preferable to the more logical conclusion," Alyson disagreed. "But unless we want to do a little digging ourselves, I say we risk a red face and let the police check it out."

"Yeah, we should call them." Mac held her hand over her nose.

Alyson used her cell phone to call 911 and the police arrived less than fifteen minutes later. After digging up the fresh grave, they discovered there was indeed a body buried there. The grave was shallow, the body unwrapped. The victim was a male, in his twenties or thirties, and dark hair was visible beneath the blood that oozed from a huge gash in his head.

"Looks like a recent murder," a detective informed them. "Probably buried no more than a few hours ago. Did any of you see anything else? Anyone lurking around?"

Alyson thought of Joseph Stillwell, then dismissed the idea. "No. Our car broke down, so we were walking home. We noticed the fresh grave and called you. We didn't see anyone."

"Do you think whoever did this is still in the area?" Mac inched closer to Trevor.

"I doubt it, but we'll have someone check it out. While you were walking around did you happen to notice anything that could have been used as the murder weapon? An ax or a shovel? Possibly even a metal pipe or a tire iron?"

"Sorry, no," Alyson, Mac, and Trevor all mumbled in turn.

"Here's my card. If you remember anything else give me a call. I'll have one of the patrolmen get your contact information, then drive you home."

"Some night, huh?" Mac groaned after the police officer had brought them back to Alyson's house.

"Tell me about it." Alyson threw a log on the fire and curled up on the floor in front of the sofa.

"Has anyone noticed that weird stuff always seems to happen to us?" Trevor asked. "What's up with that?"

"Just luck, I guess." Mac kicked off her shoes and snuggled under the comforter that had been folded over the end of the overstuffed couch.

"I wonder who he is, or more precisely who he *was*?" Trevor asked. "It seems a little coincidental that there's this big scandal going on concerning the very property where we found the body. I smell a conspiracy. Maybe old Joseph wasn't just hanging around as innocently as we thought. Maybe he didn't want people digging up his grave. Maybe he decided to take matters into his own hands."

"I don't think ghosts can actually kill people," Alyson said. "I'm pretty sure the guilty party is going to turn out to be of the human variety. Maybe once the police find out who was in the grave they can figure out who might have wanted to kill him."

Tucker, Alyson's German shepherd puppy, walked over and curled up next to her, putting his head in her lap. She absentmindedly scratched his head as she stared at the flickering flames in the old stone fireplace. "There's one thing that really bothers me about the whole thing, though. If I'm the killer and I don't want people finding out what I've done, it seems like I'd have taken more care and buried the body deeper. I mean, the way it was just barcly covered over, someone was bound to find it."

"Maybe the killer was in a hurry," Mac theorized. "Maybe the victim was just some innocent guy walking through the graveyard who happened to be in the wrong place at the wrong time and saw something he shouldn't have. The killer didn't want his secret getting out, so he whacked the intruder in the back of the head. He decided to bury him but heard someone coming so had to do it quickly."

"Yeah, but what could some innocent guy just passing through have possibly seen up in that old cemetery that would have gotten him killed?" Alyson asked. "No one ever goes up there. It's more likely he was killed somewhere else, then brought to the cemetery to be disposed of."

"Maybe the killer was just too lazy to dig a proper grave," Trevor suggested.

"You'd think if you were going to kill someone the least you could do was give them a proper burial." Mac pulled a throw pillow onto her lap and wrapped her arms around it. "Poor guy. I wonder if he lived in this area. God, I hope I didn't know him. He looked young. Don't you think he looked young? Maybe he went to our school."

"He didn't look familiar." Trevor sat down next to Mac. "I'd say he was at least in his midtwenties."

"How could you tell with all that blood? There was so much blood...Oh, God, I think I'm starting to feel sick." Mac groaned.

Trevor put his arm around her and pulled her head to his shoulder. "Don't think about it. You're going to give yourself nightmares."

"Oh, I think nightmares are a foregone conclusion at this point."

"Do you want to stay over tonight?" Alyson offered.

"No, I have a ton of chemistry homework waiting for me at home. With any luck it'll keep me up all night and nightmares won't be an issue. If that doesn't work there's always that history paper I can work on." Mac took a sip of the cider Alyson had poured for everyone when they'd first arrived. "You know, that dead body kind of looked like the new guy in our history class. Todd something."

"Birmingham," Trevor supplied. "And the body in the graveyard wasn't Todd Birmingham."

"Are you sure? They both have dark brown hair."

"I have dark brown hair," Trevor pointed out. "A lot of people have dark brown hair. It wasn't Todd Birmingham, take my word for it."

"How about Scott Ryder?"

"It wasn't Scott Ryder. I'm relatively sure it wasn't anyone we know."

"Then who was it?"

"I guess we'll find out when the police ID the guy." Alyson suddenly felt very weary. She was oh so tired of death and violence. "For now, I suggest we call a tow truck to get Raquel put to bed. There's nothing more we can do tonight and we're just going to make ourselves crazy trying to figure things out."

"Yeah, I guess you're right." Mac finished her cider and put her shoes on.

After calling a tow truck and arranging for Raquel to be taken to the local repair shop, Alyson drove the others home, then curled up with her own history paper.

Chapter 2

"Did you hear?" Chelsea asked the others as she set her books on the desk during first period the next morning. "They found some totally dead guy in the old cemetery last night."

"We heard," Mac responded. "How did you?"

"My dad's on the town council, so they called him at some ungodly hour to fill him in. It's so creepy. And with Christmas just around the corner; totally inappropriate. If someone wanted to off the guy you'd think they'd have waited until after the first of the year. To kill someone two weeks before Christmas is just plain tacky."

"Chances are the murderer didn't stop to think about how it would upset you," Mac shot back. "I'm sure he would have waited if he had."

"Well, I hope so. I'm supposed to go Christmas shopping with my mom after school. The last thing I need are serious thoughts. Buying the perfect gift requires the right mood. You need snow and decorations and sappy songs on the loudspeaker. Not thoughts of dead guys on the bluff."

"Has anyone found out the guy's identity?" Alyson asked.

"No, but my dad said he wasn't local. They think he was a transient, probably homeless. The police are doing a search of street people in the area. The theory is that he just happened to pick the wrong place to set up camp at the wrong time."

"Camp?" Trevor asked.

"Yeah. They found evidence that he was camping up there. Who'd want to camp in a graveyard? Totally creepy."

"Yeah," Mac agreed. "And it isn't exactly camping weather. The temperature's been dipping down into the thirties at night. If he was homeless wouldn't you think he'd have gone to the shelter in town?"

"A lot of homeless people would rather deal with frigid temperatures than the rigid structure of many homeless shelters." Alyson pulled her homework from her backpack as Mr. Harris walked into the room. "I'm not familiar with our local shelter, but a lot of them have rules that many homeless choose not to abide by."

"I think I'd abide by almost any rule if it meant a warm bed on a cold winter night." Mac opened her notebook and prepared to take notes.

"If I was homeless, which by the way I'd never be," Chelsea joined in, "I'd live somewhere warm, like Hawaii."

"First of all, anyone can become homeless," Mac pointed out. "Circumstances change and there are things in life you can't always control. Second of all, if you're too broke to have a place to live, how do you think you'd be able to afford to get to Hawaii?"

"I'd have Daddy fly me on his company's private jet of course."

Mac rolled her eyes as Mr. Harris's lecture began.

Alyson joined the others at their usual table for lunch in the cafeteria. Devon, her boyfriend of three months, and Eli, Devon's brother and Mac's boyfriend, had taken the last week of school before

Christmas off to join their father in Canada. Devon and Eli's dad wrote custom software for high-dollar clients and was currently working on a program for a large ski resort in the Canadian Rockies. Alyson, Mac, and Trevor were going to join them for a ski holiday the week between Christmas and New Year's. Alyson was looking forward to the vacation with her friends. Devon was leaving for college shortly after they returned home, so it would be their last opportunity to spend time together for quite a while.

"So do you want me to give you a ride tonight because your car's in the shop?" Mac asked Trevor as she unwrapped her hot roast beef sandwich.

"Ride? Were we going somewhere?"

"The meeting of the Christmas carnival, of which your mother and mine are cochairs. Boy, you really are out of it. We're supposed to help with the decorating and be assigned our jobs for next week's activities."

Mac spread apart her bun and rearranged the meat so it was more evenly distributed before adding mustard and taking a big bite.

"Activities? Of course; how could I forget? I want to go on record right now and say that I absolutely refuse to be an elf again this year," Trevor stated. "Green tights do nothing for my physique or my complexion. The guys on the team are still giving me grief about last year's costume. How about you, Alyson? You helping out? 'Cause I'm thinking green tights would match your figure and skin tone perfectly."

"Yes, I'm helping out, and no, I'm pretty sure I'm not going to be asked to be an elf. Your mother said something about working in one of the carnival booths and maybe helping with props for the annual presentation of *A Christmas Carol*. I guess we won't know for sure until we get our official assignments tonight, but I don't see green tights in my future."

"Too bad. Your talents will be wasted painting backdrops. I'll talk to my mom to see what I can do."

"Try it and die," Alyson threatened playfully.

"I'm really excited about the decorating party tonight," Mac interrupted. "Some of the local businesses have already started decorating, but once the town's decorations get put up, downtown is going to be turned into a Christmas wonderland."

"Cutter's Cove really loves its holidays, doesn't it?" Alyson observed. "I've never seen a place that goes so all out with the decorations and events."

"Yeah, we really do," Mac agreed. "And this year's carnival is especially important. The proceeds are going to go into the town's general fund to help make up for the deficit in the budget. There's a group in town that's hoping that if we can make enough money to offset next year's financial deficit, the pressure on the town council to sell the land where the old cemetery is located will be gone. Otherwise, I'm afraid we're in for a pretty nasty battle. Right now the council is divided about fifty-fifty as to whether or not to sell."

"I'm not sure I get why Psycorp wants that particular land anyway." Alyson tossed her empty yogurt container in the nearby trash bin. "There has to be some less controversial land on which to build a manufacturing plant. Besides being consecrated ground, the property is right on the ocean. You'd think there would be environmental issues even if the cemetery didn't exist."

"Yeah, the whole thing seems a little odd." Trevor gathered up his books as the bell rang to indicate the end of the period. "Maybe there's more to this seemingly innocent land acquisition than the mayor is letting on. I bet the land is sitting on a huge gold deposit. Or maybe an ancient buried treasure."

"There's no gold or treasure," Mac assured him, "but I agree that something doesn't seem quite right. Maybe we should snoop around a bit to see what we can find out."

Almost everyone in town came out for the annual decorating party. Lighted wreaths were hung from all the lampposts, garlands were strung across the street, small white lights twinkled from the branches of the trees, and huge red bows were tied on every pole or awning support that could be found. Best of all, a massive twenty-foot fir tree was decorated from top to bottom. Local vendors handed out hot cider and fresh-baked Christmas cookies, while the school band serenaded volunteers with jaunty Christmas tunes.

An ice rink was being built in the town square, and portable booths, which would be used for carnival games, were being set up around it. The lot behind the booths was reserved for the rides that would be brought in later in the week.

"Wow, this is just like Currier and Ives," Alyson admired. "All we need is snow."

"We don't get a lot of snow here. But sometimes. It'd be nice," Mac agreed.

"Where's Trevor?"

"I think I saw him on top of a really tall ladder hanging wreaths. Maybe we should find him and grab a bite to eat before the meeting. There's a vendor selling hot dogs and hamburgers and stuff near the town hall."

"I'm down with a hot dog." Alyson wrapped her cashmere-covered arm through her best friend's. "Do you guys help out with this every year?"

"Yeah, pretty much. Both my mom and Trevor's have been involved in one way or another for years. It's a huge event that, in the past, has made a lot of money for local charities. This is the first year the proceeds will be used to pad the town's budget."

"So why do you think the town has such a huge deficit this year?" Alyson waved to a girl in her history class, who was decorating the tree.

"I'm not sure. The town usually does okay as far as I know. We're a small town, but we usually have enough for basic expenses and services. Maybe it was drawing from a reserve that's all tapped out. Or it might have lost some source of outside funding. I'll have to ask my mom to see if she knows. I think that's Trevor over there by Grayson's Pharmacy, stringing garlands."

"It's too bad Devon and Eli aren't here. I think they'd really enjoy this, although skiing at a world-class resort isn't too shabby of a way to spend Christmas either."

"I know. I really miss Eli. I've been totally stressing over what to get him as a gift. I'm not sure if we're still in the casual sweater phase of if we've moved on to the more intimate gift phase. What are you getting Devon?"

"I'm definitely sticking to the less personal sweater or knit scarf. I'm trying to keep things as light and casual as possible. I mean, technically, Devon has graduated. He won't go through the ceremony until May with the rest of the seniors, but he's done with classes and will start college in another state in less than a month. I'm not even sure if we're going to try the long-distance thing or just say our good-byes after the ski trip."

"You haven't talked about it? The future, I mean?"

"That's a big no."

"Maybe you should talk to him. It'd be nice to know."

"Yeah, maybe while we're in Canada. For now, let's grab Trevor and eat. I'm starving."

After a quick dinner the trio headed over to the town hall, where the carnival assignments would be handed out. After Mac's mom reminded everyone how important this year's event was, Trevor's mom handed out pieces of paper with everyone's assignments, including times, dates, costumes, and rehearsal information.

"You're going to die." Alyson glared at Trevor as she opened her paper.

"Whatever it is I didn't do it. I swear."

"What'd ya get?" Mac asked.

"Santa's elf for the carnival and the Ghost of Christmas Past in the play. I thought I was locked into helping with the dart booth and set design. What happened?"

"Oh, there you are." Alyson's mom, Sarah, greeted her. "I hope you don't mind that I volunteered you for a couple of parts they were having trouble filling."

"Santa's elf?"

"I know, but you're a trooper, and Mac was playing the other elf, so…"

"I am?" Mac tore open her own assignment. "Santa's elf and the Ghost of Christmas Present. I'm going to kill my mom."

"Don't be hard on her. She really tried to get someone else to volunteer," Sarah explained.

"How about you, Trev? What'd you get?" Mac asked.

"What! Santa Claus and the Ghost of Christmas Future."

Mac laughed. "I guess that's what we get for having mothers who are chairwomen of the whole thing. Don't worry; you'll make a cute Santa, and I've heard that as few as ten percent of the little tykes you'll be holding on your lap actually pee."

"Very funny."

"I'm feeling a major chocolate splurge coming on. How about it, guys? Anyone up for a mocha?" Alyson asked.

"I'm in." Mac folded up her assignment sheet and put it in her pocket.

"Me too. Santa was a plump sort of guy. I guess I need to put on a little weight."

Chapter 3

Costume fittings took place the next day, after school. Trevor was fitted for a traditional Santa costume, complete with a long beard and plenty of padding. Alyson and Mac were both fitted for elf costumes, which consisted of green leggings, green pointy shoes, red and white belted dresses that were no longer than a long T-shirt, and red and green stocking caps. For her part as Christmas Past, Alyson would be dressed in a beautiful ball gown patterned from the eighteenth century, with a light green silk base and a forest green velvet overlay. For her part as Christmas Present, Mac would be dressed as a modern rocker, with a short, tight black leather skirt, a cropped red sweater, and knee-high black leather boots.

"I thought I was supposed to be the Ghost of Christmas Present. This outfit looks more like the Ghost of Christmas Sixties. No one wears stuff like this anymore." Mac tried to pull her very short skirt down past the tops of her thighs.

"Yeah, it does seem a little dated," Alyson agreed. "But it looks nice on you, sort of sexy and wild. And you have the perfect figure to pull it off."

"I don't know. I feel totally naked. This really isn't me," Mac complained.

"It's totally you," Trevor growled. "Where have you been hiding those curves all these years?"

"Under baggy sweatshirts and loose cords, where I'd prefer they stay."

"Go with it, Mac," Alyson encouraged her. "You're totally hot. It's too bad Eli isn't here. We'll have to e-mail him a photo."

"I sort of prefer you didn't."

"Come on, Mac. You're in a play. It's your chance to be someone other than who you really are." Alyson turned her friend so she was facing the full-length mirror. "See, you're gorgeous."

"But look at this sweater. When I lift my arms even a little my stomach shows. And this skirt; I don't dare bend over. I can't believe my mom actually wants me to wear this."

"I doubt your mom has even seen the costume. Mrs. Harris is in charge of the costumes," Trevor informed her. He turned Mac around in a full circle. "I for one will forever be in Mrs. Harris's debt. You're totally hot. Nothing at all like the Mac I know and love."

"Thanks a lot," Mac grumbled.

"He's just kidding." Alyson punched Trevor in the arm. "You look great, Mac; you always look great. This particular costume just makes you look different."

"I guess, but I'm going to ask Mrs. Harris if I can wear a jacket or something over it. A nice long jacket. It's December; I might get cold."

"The play is held inside the auditorium," Trevor reminded her. "I doubt frostbite will be an issue."

"You never know. Someone might leave a door open, or maybe a window. Besides, why am I the only one who has to wear such a skimpy costume? Alyson's dress has long sleeves and reaches clear to the floor and your Ghost of Christmas Future costume doesn't show even a little patch of skin. Why can't I be the Ghost of Christmas Future? I'd look good in those robes."

"There's no way I have the legs for that skirt." Trevor pushed back the hood of his costume, which completely concealed his face. "I'm sure Mrs. Harris will let you wear a jacket or something. If you're really that uncomfortable you should ask her."

Chapter 4

After school the next day Alyson, Mac, and Trevor headed over to the town hall to get their assignments for the day. There was to be a rehearsal for the play that evening, but in the meantime Mac's mom asked if they could rent a U-Haul and head over to the warehouse where the sets for the play were stored and begin bringing them back to the auditorium.

"It's a good thing we only have two more days of school before break," Alyson commented. "It looks like this carnival is going to keep us pretty busy."

"Yeah, it's a lot of work, but it's really fun." Mac, who was sitting on the bench seat between Trevor, who was driving, and Alyson, who sat shotgun, turned to face her friend. "It's the real reason we get three weeks for winter break instead of the more traditional two. The carnival has been a town tradition since I was a kid. It wouldn't feel like Christmas without it."

"Speaking of Christmas, you guys get your tree yet?" Trevor asked.

Mac shook her head. "No. My mom's been totally busy cochairing. How about you?"

"My mom asked me if I'd pick one up. She wanted to have it so the family could decorate it before the weekend, when things get really busy. We could deliver the props, then go by one of the lots to pick up a couple of trees. How about you, Aly? Need a tree?"

"I guess. We don't have one yet. We usually have a service get us one."

"A service?" Trevor asked.

"Yeah, you know, a decorating service."

"You're kidding, right? You don't decorate your own tree?" Trevor asked.

"Let's go to Dooley's Farm and cut our own," Mac suggested, quickly changing the subject. "I'll call my mom to make sure it's okay that I get the tree without the rest of the family, but she'll probably be glad for the help."

"You really cut your own tree?" Alyson asked.

"Yeah, almost every year. It's sort of a Reynolds family tradition. Normally, we'd all go together, but this year Mom is really in hyperdrive over the carnival."

Alyson watched as Trevor turned off the highway onto a side road that was used to access the buildings in the industrial section of town.

"Here we are." Trevor pulled up in front of one of the whitewashed warehouses, where the decorations were stored. "Aly, why don't you jump out and open the door and I'll back in?"

Alyson took the key Mac's mother had given her and opened the heavy rolling door. "Uh, Trev," she yelled as Trevor swung the truck around to get into position to back in, "you'd better check this out. I think we have a problem."

Mac and Trevor climbed out of the truck and joined Alyson near the entrance of the warehouse, which housed dozens of smaller storage units. The interior of the town's unit had been totally trashed.

"Oh my God. What happened?" Mac gasped.

"My mom's going to freak." Trevor shook his head. "Who would do something like this?"

"And why?" Mac started to walk deeper into the storage unit. "This makes no sense."

"When was the last time anyone was here to check on things?" Alyson asked.

"Last year, as far as I know, when everything was packed away after the carnival," Trevor answered.

Alyson walked over to the rolling door and looked at the lock she had just opened. "It doesn't look like anyone tampered with the lock. Whoever did this must have had a key."

"That can't be." Mac joined her. "As far as I know, there's only one key and they keep it locked up in town hall. The only people who would have access to it are the town council and maybe some staff. Why would any of them do this?"

"I don't know, but there's no sign of forced entry. We'd better call your mom." Alyson got her cell phone from her purse and handed it to Mac.

"I'm not calling her. She's going to freak. It's only three days until the carnival starts and ten days until the play. The sets are totally destroyed. What are we going to do?"

"Not to worry." Alyson tried to comfort her friend. "We'll figure something out. We'll call Caleb. He's a genius at this sort of thing. I'm sure he can rally some of his artsy buddies and they can rebuild the sets in no time."

Caleb Wellington was a fellow Seacliff High student who was in charge of props for the school's events.

"It looks like a total loss." Trevor had been checking out the contents of the storage unit and joined the others. "Someone went all Rambo on the place. Best I can tell, someone with a chain saw chopped all the backdrops to pieces. I doubt anything is salvageable. We have to let someone know."

"I'm not calling my mom. You call yours."

Trevor took out his own cell phone and let it ring. "She's not answering. I guess you'll have to call yours."

"Okay, but if she has a complete meltdown don't say I didn't warn you. She's already a little intense about this whole carnival thing."

Mac called Caleb first to ask for his help in rebuilding the sets in time for the play. He agreed to gather some of his friends together and get started right away. Then she called her mom and filled her in on the bad news.

"It was smart of you to get Caleb's promise of help before calling your mom," Alyson complimented Mac. "It allowed you to soften the blow with some good news."

"Yeah, and it was nice of Caleb to agree to help out, and the props he builds will probably be a lot better than the old, worn-out ones we've been using for years, but this is really a setback for the carnival committee." Mac climbed into the truck next to Trevor after making her calls and securing the rolling door. "We were really hoping to have a killer profit to donate to the town, but the cost of buying wood and paint for the new sets is going to cut into that."

Trevor put his arm around Mac's shoulders. "We'll make up the difference. This year's carnival is going to be the best one ever. Now, let's go get those trees we promised to bring home. I'm thinking a twelve-footer."

"But you have an eight-foot ceiling," Mac reminded him. "Alyson, on the other hand, could put a huge tree in her entry. At least a fifteen-footer."

"The problem is," Alyson realized, "I don't have any decorations. I'm not sure how I'm going to decorate a two-foot tree, little alone a fifteen-foot one."

"You don't have any decorations?" Trevor asked. "No Styrofoam bulbs covered in glitter that you made in the first grade, or red and green paper chains you glued together yourself?"

"No, nothing. Our box of decorations got lost in the move," she improvised.

"We'll head over to the Holiday Store downtown after we get the trees and take the truck back. They'll have everything you need," Mac suggested.

The pumpkin patch at Dooley's Farm had been transformed into a tree farm in the two months since they'd been there to pick up pumpkins for the haunted hayride. Alyson discovered that obtaining a tree from the farm was a little more complicated than just selecting one from a lot. First you had to trudge over the muddy hillside in search of the perfect specimen and then you had to cut it down with an ax the farm provided, and finally you had to haul it down the hillside to your vehicle. The process of obtaining three perfect trees took longer than anyone had anticipated and the winter sun had already slipped beyond the horizon by the time they finished.

"I'm starving," Trevor said as they loaded the last tree. "All that chopping and carrying really worked up my appetite. How about we drop these trees off and take the truck back, then get something to eat before heading over to the Holiday Store? They should be open late this time of year."

"Sounds good to me," Mac agreed. "Dinners at our house lately have been of the frozen food variety."

After dropping the trees at everyone's house and bringing the truck back to the rental lot, they stopped by the carnival admin center to fill their mothers in on their plans to have dinner out.

"Oh, good. You're here," Mac's mom greeted them. "I need you to take the rental truck and drive to Portland to pick up the wood and supplies for the new set. Caleb and his gang are going to start on it tomorrow."

"But we already returned the truck," Mac informed her. "We were just heading out to get something to eat."

"I'm sorry, but you'll have to get the truck back. I'll call over to the rental place to explain the situation. You can grab a burger on the way."

"Sure, no problem," Alyson agreed. "Can you tell my mom what we're doing? I know she's around here somewhere."

"She's helping to organize the prizes for the carnival booths. I'm heading over there anyway, so I'll let her know. You guys will need to hurry. The lumberyard is staying open late for us and I don't want to keep them waiting longer than we have to."

"Okay, we're gone. Where do you want us to drop the lumber?" Trevor asked.

"Just leave it in the truck for tonight. Caleb is going to see if we can use the art room at the school to build the sets. If it's all right you can take the supplies over there tomorrow."

They grabbed burgers, fries, and shakes from Joey's Burger Joint, then headed over to the rental lot to pick up the truck they'd just returned. The drive to Portland was grueling at this time of day. By the time they arrived at the lumberyard, which was on the other side of the city, it was quite late. They loaded the supplies, then started out for the long ride back to Cutter's Cove.

"I've been thinking about the destroyed sets," Alyson said as they drove through the dark countryside. "You said the town council and staff would have access to the warehouse key. Maybe someone who favored the sale of the land destroyed the sets as a way to hurt the town financially."

"I don't know," Mac mused. "At this point half the council seems to support the sale, but I think that's only because they feel they have no choice. I don't think anyone would want to sell the land if they didn't have to. It seems like everyone on the council supports the carnival and hopes it's a huge success so they won't have to deal with the controversy a sale of the land to Psycorp would cause."

"It was just a thought. The list of suspects is going to be somewhat limited because there were no signs of forced entry. Is there anyone on the council who might be holding a grudge? It could be anyone who's worked for the town in the past year."

"We can ask around tomorrow," Mac suggested. "Maybe we should have called the police. Whoever broke into the warehouse might have left fingerprints."

"I'm sure someone from the carnival committee thought to notify the police," Trevor joined in.

"If not we'll call them tomorrow," Alyson said. "Right now I just want to get this stuff dropped off and get home to bed before it's time to get up for school."

"I hear ya." Mac sighed

Chapter 5

Wednesday was their last full day of school before winter break, with Thursday only a half day before they'd be off until after the first of the year. The carnival was set to open for its weeklong engagement on Friday night. Although the play wasn't due to open until the following weekend, there was a lot to do to get ready—lines to learn, sets to build, and costumes to finish.

"I can't believe I'm saying this," Mac said with a yawn as she picked at her sandwich during fifth-period lunch, "but I'm actually looking forward to December 23 and the end of the carnival. My mom has turned into some sort of holiday Godzilla. I know she's under a lot of pressure, but the carnival hasn't even started and my entire family is walking on eggshells for fear of setting her off over some little thing."

"I know what you mean," Trevor agreed. "I'm mostly trying to stay out of the line of fire. Things should get better once the carnival actually starts, though. It's the week leading up to the opening that's the worst."

"Is it like this every year?" Alyson asked as she opened her diet cola.

"Not really," Mac answered. "This is the first time my mom has had so much responsibility. She helps out every year, but Mrs. Larson has been chairwoman for as long as I can remember."

"So why isn't Mrs. Larson running things this year?" Alyson wondered.

"She moved to Boca to be close to her sister and her family. Mr. Larson passed away last year. He'd been sick for a while, and I think Mrs. Larson needed a complete change. She was a neighbor and had confided in my mom that she was concerned about the carnival, so my mom and Trevor's agreed to pitch in and take over. I don't think they had any idea how much work it would be. Mrs. Larson always made it look so easy. Of course, she didn't have to deal with slashed budgets and destroyed props."

"It was really nice of your moms to step up like that." Alyson stirred her nonfat yogurt. "Not a lot of people would have."

"Mrs. Larson was a nice woman who'd been through a tough time." Mac opened her eyes and leaned forward onto her elbows. "My mom said it gave her peace of mind to move on, knowing that the carnival was in good hands."

After school they headed into town, parking in the vacant lot near town hall and heading off on foot in search of their mothers and their assignments for the day. Carnival headquarters was a complete zoo, as was to be expected. People were running to and fro giving commands, looking for lost items, and complaining in elevated voices about one problem or another.

Trevor's mother was on the phone, arguing with someone on the other end, and Alyson and Mac's mothers were nowhere to be found. Deciding to wait to speak to her rather than going in search of the others, they took a seat on a long bench someone had shoved up against a wall. After several animated minutes and a string of very unholidayish profanities, Trevor's mother finally hung up.

"If it's not one thing it's another," she complained. "I was just talking with someone at the newspaper in Portland. The carnival ad I spent hours writing never ran. They insisted someone called to cancel it. Of course they didn't have the name of the person. Now the soonest they can run the ad is in Friday's edition. That's not going to give the out-of-towners much notice for this weekend's activities. I'm sure it's going to hurt our turnout."

"I'm sure it'll be fine, Mom," Trevor tried to comfort her. "Everyone in town will come out for opening weekend, so I'm sure we'll have a crowd. Last year you could barely get through the area where the rides were set up. What's on tap for the weekend anyway?"

"On Friday night there's the tree lighting in the town square and caroling by local school groups. Immediately after that there'll be the opening ceremony and the Santa house will be open. Saturday we have the rides and games as well as the Santa house. I have three sets of helpers, so everyone can trade off. Saturday night there's the children's pageant in the auditorium. I really should check with Nancy Baker, the pageant coordinator, to make sure everything is on track for that. Sunday we have the holiday concert. Joanna Crawford is in charge of that. If you kids see her let her know I need to speak to her about the programs for the concert."

"What do you need us to do today?" Trevor asked.

"You have play rehearsal in a few hours, but for now I guess you can find Mackenzie's mom and help her. I think I saw her heading over to the school to check on the progress of the set design."

They headed back over to the school, which they had just left. "It's too bad we didn't know we were supposed to help Caleb before we went all the way into town," Mac groused.

"Don't you guys think it's strange that someone supposedly called and canceled the newspaper ad?" Alyson asked. "I mean, first the set was destroyed and now the ad was canceled. It's looking more and more like someone is trying to sabotage the carnival."

"But who would do that?" Mac asked.

"I don't know, but things seem awfully suspicious. I think we should keep our eyes open. I have a bad feeling."

By the time they caught up with Caleb he was up to his ears in partially painted sets, sawdust, and enthusiastic helpers. As usual, he was completely in charge and seemed to know exactly what needed to be done. He had quite a reputation for his set designs and props; most recently, he'd designed all the props for the haunted hayride, which had been a huge success.

"Hey, guys. What's up?" he asked as he continued to draw the outline for the next set to be cut out.

"We're supposed to be looking for my mom," Mac informed him.

"You just missed her. She got a call about a missing shipment of some kind and took off."

"A missing shipment?" Alyson asked.

"Yeah. She seemed pretty frantic. Seems like the carnival committee is having their share of problems this year."

"Do you think you'll have the sets for the play done on time?" Trevor asked.

"It'll be tight, but barring complications we should be ready for opening night a week from Saturday."

"I guess we should go find my mom to see if we can help with her current crisis," Mac said.

Once again they headed downtown to carnival central. When they asked around for Mac's mother they found out she was over at the Cutter's Cove Community Church kitchen, where the food that would be sold throughout the carnival would be prepared. The original church was a small A-frame that had been built in the midnineteenth century. Over the years the building had been enlarged, and an auditorium, with an industrial-size kitchen, a professional stage, and a storage room for hundreds of folding chairs had been added. Almost all the town events were held there.

"Reverend Thompson, have you seen my mom?" Mac asked when he greeted them from the garden in front of the main entrance of the church.

"She's over in the kitchen. It seems a delivery she was expecting never showed up and she's quite frantic. I thought I'd come out here to tend the garden. I'm sure, when all is said and done, your good mother wouldn't have wanted me to be witness to her colorful language. The carnival does seem to bring out the dark side of folks."

"Don't blame her," Mac defended her mom. "All kinds of things have gone wrong. I think everyone's nerves are on edge. We'll go see if we can help."

As they walked through the auditorium doors they saw a large group of people sitting around as if they didn't know what to do, while Mac's mom's voice could be heard from the kitchen, talking to someone on the phone.

"How does a truck disappear?" she articulated clearly and loudly. "Well, I suggest you do. Call me back when you find it."

"Something wrong?" Mac asked as her frazzled-looking mother hung up the phone.

"I have twenty volunteers sitting around who are supposed to be making candy for the carnival, but I just found out the shipment of supplies I ordered never showed up. The store I ordered them from insists the truck started out on schedule, but it never arrived, and the driver isn't answering his cell phone or radio. They're looking into it, but in the meantime I have a crowd of volunteers with nothing to do."

"Maybe we could go over to the market to get the things you need," Mac suggested.

"They won't have anywhere near the quantity we need. I ordered the stuff from an outlet in Portland a month ago. I don't know what we'll do if the truck doesn't show up."

The phone on the wall in the kitchen rang.

"Cutter's Cove Community Church," Mac's mom jumped to answer it. "Oh, God, you're kidding."

"What is it?" Mac asked as soon as her mother hung up.

"The delivery truck was in an accident just outside of town. Someone ran the poor man off the road, then took off. The driver is in an ambulance, on the way to the hospital. The woman I talked to said the highway patrol reported that the back of the truck is intact and that I could send someone out to pick up the supplies. Do you kids mind going?"

"No, not at all. I hope the driver's going to be okay." Mac hugged her mom. "We'll be back in a jiffy. We haven't returned the rental truck yet, so we'll take that."

Once again they climbed into the cab of the rental truck and headed out of town.

"Okay, now I know something weird's going on," Alyson insisted. "First the sets, then the ad, now this. These things are way too coincidental to be coincidences."

"I have to agree," Mac said. "I don't *want* to agree, but I have to. Who would do such a thing?"

"I say we go into research mode," Trevor said. "We've solved mysteries before; we can solve this one."

"Yeah, but when?" Alyson asked. "By the time we deliver the candy supplies it'll be time for rehearsal."

"We've got a twenty-minute drive to where the truck was hit and another thirty-minute drive back into town." Mac pulled a small notebook from her purse. "Let's start brainstorming."

"Good idea." Alyson nodded. "We know the set for the play was destroyed sometime between the time it was put away last year and yesterday. It doesn't appear there was a forced entry, so we have to guess it was an inside job."

"Then my mom's ad was canceled and it looks like the truck carrying the supplies for the candy was ambushed," Trevor added.

"That all adds up to someone wanting to sabotage the carnival," Mac concluded. "But who would want to do that and why?"

"Someone from Psycorp," Trevor deduced. "They want to buy the land, and if the carnival is a big enough success maybe the town will have enough money so it won't have to sell."

"Makes sense," Alyson agreed. "But how'd they get into the warehouse?"

"Maybe they bribed one of the town staff," Mac jumped in. "They'd need someone on the inside to know what was going on with the carnival anyway. How else would they have known about the ad or the delivery truck? They're all the way back east. They must have someone in Cutter's Cove working with a local perp to orchestrate the sabotages."

"Wow, Mac, you're really getting into this detective stuff," Alyson commented. "You've really gotten the lingo down."

"So now what?" Trevor asked.

"We could make a list of everyone who might have access to the key to the storage unit," Mac suggested.

"I think we should check out Psycorp," Alyson said. "Mac can get on the Net to see what she can find out about them. If they're the bad guys, why do they want that particular piece of property so bad? I mean, there have to be other parcels in this area they could build on. If they're in on the sabotage there must be a reason they'd go to so much trouble."

"I think we're here." Trevor pulled over. "The cab of the truck is really banged up. I hope the driver's okay."

"Who'd do something like this just to sabotage a local carnival?" Mac asked. "If this was intentional we're dealing with some pretty dangerous people."

"Let's get started moving the supplies," Trevor said. "It's going to take a while."

After transferring all the salvageable supplies from the delivery truck to the rental one, they turned around and headed back to town. The candy-making volunteers were left to unload everything when they got back to the church; Alyson, Mac, and Trevor were already late for play rehearsal.

"That was really fun," Mac said as they left the auditorium two hours later. "I was dreading having such a big part in the play, but it's turned out to be a real hoot. Maybe I'll pursue a career in acting after graduation."

"Nothing against your stellar performance," Alyson retorted, "but a redirect to acting would be a huge loss to the technology community. With your brain, you need to be a scientist or a software designer or something."

"Yeah, I guess. But I could always act in my spare time."

"I think nuclear physics is pretty intense. I doubt you'll have much free time," Trevor commented.

"Hey, I never said I was going into nuclear physics."

"Yeah, but it'll be something like that. Let's face it, Mac, you're destined to live a big life."

"For now, though, you're just one of us: one of the little guys. Enjoy it while you can." Alyson slipped her arm through Mac's. "Doing important things for important people in exotic places can wait. For now, I say we get pizza. I'm starved."

"Pirates Pizza it is." Trevor climbed into the passenger side of Mac's bright orange Volkswagen Bug.

"Actually, I was thinking about getting takeout." Alyson dug out the keys to her four-door Jeep. "Tucker's been home alone a lot this week. I thought we could spend some quality time with him while we eat. Then maybe we could use Mac's laptop to check out Psycorp."

"We'll pick up a pizza, then meet you at your house," Mac said. "A combo okay?"

"A combo's perfect," Alyson answered.

Alyson couldn't help but think of the previous Christmas as she drove home. A year ago she was still Amanda Parker, an heiress living in a penthouse apartment and attending a private girls' school. She'd never even heard of Cutter's Cove and now she found herself an integral part of the annual holiday celebration.

Tucker danced around Alyson as she walked in the front door when she arrived home. He almost tripped her in his enthusiasm. "Hey, boy. You miss me?"

Tucker barked once in response as he continued to wag his whole body. "Just let me put my stuff down and change into something warmer and we'll go out for a quick run." Alyson set her purse on the secretary in the entry hall. She went upstairs to change into her sweats and running shoes and then headed out with the energetic German shepherd running along beside her toward the cliffs overlooking the Pacific Ocean.

Alyson loved her new home. She'd moved here with her mom in August, after the murder of her best friend had caused her to flee New York and the life she had always known. At first the thought of entering witness protection and creating a whole new life had frightened her, but now she was happier than she had ever been before.

She'd met Mac and Trevor on the first day of school, and the three of them quickly became best friends. It had been a busy and interesting few months ever since. They seemed to constantly be drawn into one mystery after another.

Tucker ran back and forth across the narrow path as he expended his pent-up puppy energy. Alyson felt bad that he'd been home alone so much this week, but once the school break began she'd start bringing Tucker downtown with her.

"Come on, Tucker, let's go home. I think I just saw the guys pull up. They brought pizza. Maybe we'll give you a piece."

Tucker jogged happily home, enthusiastically running up to greet Mac and Trevor when they pulled up. After petting him and offering him the proper amount of attention, they all went indoors to eat and start their research.

"What'd you find?" Alyson asked Mac, who was sitting on the floor, her computer on the coffee table in front of a roaring fire.

"Well, I know Psycorp isn't a publicly traded company; I haven't found records of any financial information or credit rating on file. In fact, I haven't found anything at all. What state are they from?"

"I don't know." Alyson tucked her feet up under her as she curled into the large overstuffed sofa her mom had recently bought. "All I remember anyone saying is back east. I guess that could mean anything."

The music in the background switched to the soft melody of Christmas piano as Mac continued to work. Alyson stared at the flickering flames from the candles on the mantel as she tried to remember whether anyone had ever mentioned a state.

"I see you haven't decorated your tree yet," Trevor commented as Mac worked. "It looks great in the entry, but it's kind of naked."

"I still haven't had a chance to get over to the Holiday Store. Maybe tomorrow. I'd like to pick up some garlands for the banister and maybe a poinsettia or two."

"My house looks like Santa moved his workshop to Cutter's Cove. Every surface, nook, and cranny is fully decorated," Mac told them. "My mom and sisters have been unpacking the fifty or so boxes of decorations we've accumulated over the years ever since we dropped off the tree."

"When does your mom have time to decorate?" Alyson asked. "Every time I've been downtown she's been there."

"I think the holidays are kind of like a drug to her. She has all this energy and needs very little sleep. She baked a batch of cookies before I even got up this morning."

"Wow, good for her." Alyson snuggled back into the soft cushions of the sofa. "Although I think I prefer a mellower holiday—soft lights, soft music, hot cocoa in front of a roaring fire."

"I think it's the sugar." Mac continued to type in commands as she spoke. "She starts baking the day after Thanksgiving and then goes into hyperdrive until after the first of the year. I can't find any information on Psycorp at all. Didn't the mayor insinuate that they were a large company? There should be something about them."

"I guess we could ask him about them tomorrow," Trevor suggested. "He's been helping out with the carnival preparations, so I'm sure he'll be around."

"Yeah, I guess." Mac squinted as she continued to try different search engines. "Hmm, that's interesting."

"What?" Alyson got up and walked over to the coffee table in front of which Mac was sitting.

"The only address on file for them is a post office box and it's right here in Portland, not anywhere on the East Coast."

"Are you sure it's the same company?" Trevor asked.

"It's the only Psycorp listed. Why would they say they had a large presence back east if they're a local company? And if they are local, and supposedly a large, wealthy company, why haven't we heard of them before?"

"Something isn't adding up," Trevor stated.

"Maybe we're missing something," Alyson said. "Maybe Psycorp is only part of their name and that's why nothing is coming up."

"I guess." Mac sounded unconvinced.

Trevor was shaking his head. "I don't know. It's been my experience that if something walks like a duck, it's usually a duck. If things look suspicious there's usually a reason why."

"Trevor's right," Mac agreed. "Something's not jiving. For there to be basically no information available on a company that supposedly has the resources to buy an expensive piece of land and build a large factory doesn't fit. I mean, does anyone even remember what this company manufactures?"

"Actually, no, but I'm sure the mayor must have said at some point," Alyson supposed.

"There's absolutely no further information available on the company, and no address other than the post office box. Not even a phone number." Mac continued typing. "Hang on, let me check something." Her fingers flew over the keyboard. "Now that's interesting."

"What?" Alyson asked.

"Psycorp didn't file incorporation papers until two months ago."

"Then that can't be the same company," Alyson concluded. "There must be more to the name, like maybe Psycorp Manufacturing or Psycorp Industries. Maybe that's why nothing's coming up."

"I input search parameters that would pull up anything with the word Psycorp anywhere in the name, and this one company is all that popped up."

"Are you sure you have the spelling right?" Trevor got up from the sofa and went to stand behind Mac.

"Pretty sure. I mean, I've never seen the word written down before, but based on the way it sounds I'd say this is the way to spell it."

"Maybe the mayor can clear things up." Alyson threw another log on the fire, then walked toward the kitchen. "In the meantime, who's up for hot cocoa? My mom bought some of those little marshmallows and everything."

Chapter 6

School let out at noon on Thursday, and they headed downtown early. After grabbing deli sandwiches at the sub shop, they went over to the mayor's office to see if they could get some answers to their questions regarding Psycorp.

"We'd like a minute with the mayor if he's available," Alyson addressed the middle-aged woman behind the reception desk at town hall.

"Do you have an appointment?"

"No, but we were hoping for just a few minutes of his time."

"Can I ask what this is regarding?"

"We have a few questions about the proposed sale of the land where the old cemetery is located."

"I'll check to see if he's available." The secretary walked through the door behind her, leaving them to wait.

"I hope he'll see us," Mac whispered.

Alyson watched as the second hand of a wall clock made a full revolution.

The secretary finally returned. "He'll see you now."

"Mayor Gregor," Alyson said, holding out her hand to the stout man behind the desk. "I'm Alyson Prescott, and these are my friends, Mackenzie Reynolds and Trevor Johnson."

"I've seen you three around, helping out with the carnival. It's nice to see young people who are so community service–oriented. Care for a mint?" He held out a candy dish filled with pastel-colored candies.

"No, thank you." Alyson sat down on one of the chairs on the other side of the mayor's desk.

He set the bowl back down on his desk. "What can I do for you?"

"We wanted to ask you a few questions about Psycorp. The company that's trying to buy the old cemetery," Alyson added when he didn't immediately respond.

"And why might that be?" The mayor leaned back in his chair, scrutinizing his guests.

"We're working on an article for the school newspaper," Alyson improvised. "We were interested in learning more about the company: where exactly they're located, what they manufacture, why they're interested in locating a facility in Cutter's Cove. That sort of thing."

"And why would the school be interested in an article about Psycorp? In my day the school newspaper focused on things like sports and cafeteria food."

"We're trying to branch out to cover subjects that affect our community," Alyson answered. "Psycorp is interested in becoming part of our community, so we thought it was relevant."

"Why are you working on this now? Isn't school out for the winter holiday?"

"Well, yes, but our deadline is shortly after we get back, so we decided to get a jump on our research."

"I see. I'm rather busy right now, but Sue Hein from the town clerk's office should be able to provide you with a company bio. Her office is closed for lunch right now, but you can come back after one thirty."

"We'll do that. Thank you for your time. Oh, by the way," Alyson said, turning back toward the mayor as they neared the door, "what state did you say Psycorp operates in?"

"Everything will be in the company bio. Now I really must make a call." The mayor picked up the phone on his desk.

"He seemed pretty tight-lipped about Psycorp," Trevor said softly as they left his office. "Could be he's hiding something."

"Personally, I just don't think he wanted to be bothered," Mac countered. "I'm surprised he agreed to see us at all. It's not like we can vote or anything."

"So what now?" Trevor asked. "The clerk's office won't open for another half hour."

"I guess we could go check in with our moms to see what they have planned for us this afternoon," Mac said. "The carnival officially opens tomorrow evening, so I'm sure they'll have something."

They headed to carnival headquarters, where Mac greeted her mother and kissed her on the cheek. "We came by to see what you needed us to do today."

"I'm glad you're here. I could really use someone to decorate the inside of the auditorium. Here's a key to the closet near the kitchen. You should find everything you need in there. Oh, and why don't you stop by to pick up your costumes? I was told the alterations have been completed."

"Sure; anything else?"

"The auditorium will take you most of the afternoon, but if you finish early enough to help out with anything else before rehearsal, come find me. I have an endless list."

"Okay." Mac closed her hand around the key. "See ya."

"So Santa, are you ready for your big debut tomorrow night?" Alyson asked as they walked toward the auditorium.

"I guess. I just hope no one from the football team sees me. I'll never live it down."

"*You'll* never live it down." Mac sighed. "What about me? I'm the one who has to run around half naked the whole week. That elf outfit leaves little to the imagination and the one for the Ghost of Christmas Present is downright indecent."

"Yeah, I can't wait to see you in them." Trevor wiggled his eyebrows. "If I had my way, all our rehearsals would be dress rehearsals."

"Geez, is your mind always in the gutter?"

"Pretty much."

"God, guys are so emotionally retarded." Mac stormed off toward the auditorium.

"Listen, hormone boy, you might want to tone things down a bit before Mac bruises that pretty face of yours," Alyson warned him.

"I know. I just love to yank her chain. She's always wearing those offbeat baggy clothes and she has such a great body; it's nice to see her in something hot for once."

"Do I detect a lustful interest?"

"Na. Mac's been my best friend since kindergarten. My teasing is lust-free. I promise," Trevor insisted, offering a Boy Scout salute.

"Well, if you want to stay best friends you might want to watch it. Mac's really self-conscious. I think your teasing might push her too far."

"Okay." Trevor raised his hands in surrender. "Backing off."

They picked up their costumes, then went in search of the closet that held the decorations.

"My mom said it was near the kitchen; this must be it." Mac unlocked the door and pulled it open. "Except it's empty. Does anyone see another closet?"

Alyson looked around. "No, this is it. Maybe someone already picked them up. Let's ask around."

They asked everyone, but no one had seen the decorations.

"We'll have to go ask my mom." Mac groaned. "If something happened to the decorations I'd hate to be too close to the fallout. She had two pots of coffee before she left the house this morning and she was drinking a cup when we checked in with her. Decoration emergencies and caffeine overload really don't mix."

After they delivered the bad news to Mrs. Reynolds a thorough search for the decorations was organized, but nothing showed up. After a fair amount of ranting and the spewing of language from her normally emotionally stable mother that made Mac blush, it was decided that Mrs. Reynolds would call ahead to the store manager to provide a list and Alyson, Trevor, and Mac would go to the Holiday Store to pick up new decorations.

Alyson found the store quaint and charming. There was an electric Christmas train circling most of the store, and a Victorian village had been set up in the window, complete with tiny people, farm animals, and Santa's sleigh. Dozens of trees covered in white lights had been set up throughout the store, showing off the various ornaments available for sale. "Frosty the Snowman" played on a continuous loop over the loudspeaker as dozens of people shopped.

As the others picked up Mrs. Reynolds's order, Alyson filled her basket with white lights, a variety of ornaments in differing sizes and colors, garlands for the fireplace and stairway, red scented candles, and a wreath for the front door. These decorations would be modest compared to what the decorator her mom had always hired turned out, but this year everything would be personal, and she couldn't remember ever being so excited about Christmas before.

They loaded everything in Alyson's Jeep, then headed back to the auditorium to begin the huge task of stringing almost a hundred sets of twinkle lights. By the time they'd finished it was time to head over to play rehearsal.

"Darn," Mac said as she waited for her part to come up. "We forgot to go back to the town clerk's office for the company bio on Psycorp."

Alyson looked at her watch. "They'll be closed by now. We'll have to go tomorrow. We don't have school, so we can go first thing. Oh, I'm up. Wish me luck."

Rehearsals dragged on past the normally allotted two hours because pretty much everyone seemed to forget their lines. By the time they finally left the auditorium it was late and most of the cars were gone from the lot. Alyson's Jeep was parked at the auditorium because they'd used it to go to the store, but Trevor and Mac's cars were still in the lot at town hall.

"Jump in; I'll give you a ride to your cars," Alyson offered.

"Thanks. I'm bushed." Mac got in the back while Trevor climbed in the front.

"I hope no one expects us to be here too early tomorrow." Mac closed her eyes and leaned back against the seat behind her. "If the next eight days are as hectic as the last few, I think sleep deprivation is going to become an issue."

"I know what you mean." Trevor yawned.

"Here we are." Alyson stopped her Jeep in front of Mac and Trevor's cars.

"See you in the morning." Trevor hopped out and walked around to the driver's side of his Ford. "Oh, God, Raquel. What have they done to you?"

"Trev, what's wrong?" Alyson shifted the Jeep into park and jumped out to see what he was moaning about.

The letters *M-Y-O-B* had been painted in bright red on the side of his shiny black Mustang.

"Who would do such a thing?" Mac stared, stunned.

"And why Raquel?" Trevor groaned. "I just got her back from the shop and still have to finish paying off that bill. It'll take a year's allowance to have her repainted."

"We must be getting close to something someone doesn't want us to find out," Alyson surmised.

"The mayor," Mac deduced.

"Maybe. Or maybe he mentioned to the clerk that we'd be stopping by, or maybe his secretary. We need to make a list of everyone who could be a suspect and work from there."

"I'm with Alyson." Trevor looked like he might cry as he caressed the door of his beloved car. "Whoever did this to Raquel must die."

"Death might be a bit drastic, but I agree that someone should pay. My place is the closest," Mac offered as her fatigue gave way to fury. "We can go over there to make the list. My sisters should be in bed already, so it might not be too crazy."

Mac's family lived in a nice but modest tract house in an older neighborhood close to downtown. The large front lawn was decorated with mechanical snowmen waving to passing cars, a mechanical Santa in a large red sleigh being pulled by brightly lit reindeer, and jolly elves positioned around gaily wrapped packages. Colorful red, orange, yellow, blue, and green lights had been strung along the roof, and a large evergreen wreath with a huge red bow graced the front door.

The inside of the house was decorated no less lavishly. The tree they'd cut just a few days before was densely decorated with colorful lights, shiny red balls, and tons of homemade ornaments from Christmases past. A small train circled the tree, weaving in and out of strategically placed presents.

The mantel was decorated with red candles, angel figurines, and boughs of holly. Six hand-knit stockings hung from ceramic stocking holders, three on each side of the fireplace opening. The remnants of a fire still smoldered, filling the room with cozy warmth.

"Wow, this really does look like Santa's workshop." Alyson picked up one of the Wise Men from a large nativity scene laid out on a table near the sofa. "It must take forever to set all this stuff up each year. And taking it down; now that must be a real drag. But I like it; it feels cozy. Like a real home should."

"My mom does most of the work, but we all usually help out with the tree. My dad does the outside stuff. He used to decorate the roof, but after a nasty slip during an early winter storm a few years ago, my mom made him stick to the lawn."

Mac walked into the kitchen, which was just as decorated as the living room. She found a yellow legal pad in a drawer near the phone and set it on the table, which was covered with a bright red cloth. Then she took out several homemade cookies from the Santa cookie jar and arranged them on a "Night Before Christmas" plate.

"These are really good. My mom made them this morning," Mac informed her friends. "We may as well have a snack while we work. I'll get some milk. Alyson, why don't you start the list?"

"Let's start with the first incident," Alyson suggested. "The destroyed props. Who would have had access to the key and, even more important, who would have known where the sets were stored? I mean, there's no reason to believe every town employee would have access to that information."

"Well, the mayor's secretary would probably know." Mac set a pitcher of cold milk and three glasses next to the plate of cookies. "I assume she keeps track of the mayor's notes and filings."

"How about the bookkeeper who wrote the check to rent the storage unit?" Alyson asked.

"The mayor and town council usually need to approve any expenditures. They probably approved the expense in the first place," Trevor said.

"Okay, so we have the mayor and his secretary, the other five town council members, and the bookkeeper." Alyson made added them to the list. "Anyone else?

"The town clerk had the key," Mac reminded her.

"Okay, I'll add her. The next thing that happened was the canceled ad. Would all of those people have had access to information concerning the ad?"

"Probably," Trevor guessed. "But maybe we should consider motive. Which of those people have come out as opposed to the sale? It makes sense that if you opposed the sale you'd want the carnival to be a success, so it wouldn't be in your best interest to sabotage it."

"Let me see the list," Mac said, holding out her hand.

Alyson handed over the list and a pen and then helped herself to one of the gooey cookies.

"I know Mr. Jordan, Mrs. White, and Mrs. Forester all oppose the sale." Mac crossed off their names. "The mayor, Mr. Green, and Dr. Went all seemed to support it. I have no idea where the staff stands, so we'll leave them on the list for now."

"That narrows our suspects down to six people. What about the incident with the truck?" Alyson took a small bite of the cookie and chewed it appreciatively. "That was pretty violent. I don't know any of these people. Do you think any of them seem likely to do such a thing?"

"I don't know any of them very well," Mac answered. "Mr. Green is Chelsea's dad; I hope it isn't him. Dr. Went is a dentist. He seems nice enough. Both of them are well off financially. If our theory holds true that someone from Cutter's Cove is being bribed to help someone at Psycorp disrupt the carnival, it seems it would be one of the staff."

"Besides, whoever molested poor Raquel probably did it as a reaction to our visit to the mayor. It tracks that it would be staff. Maybe it was the mayor himself, although it seems a childish thing for him to do. He usually presents himself as being pretty sophisticated."

"His secretary doesn't seem the type either," Alyson said. "Besides, whomever vandalized your car had to have known it was yours, and I'm not sure she would have."

"I'm not sure why the bookkeeper would have even known about our visit," Mac pointed out. "We weren't asking for money. It seems more likely it would be the mayor, his secretary, or possibly the town clerk, if the mayor happened to mention we would be stopping by for the company bio."

"It looks like several people had the opportunity. We just need to figure out who had a motive. Let's just keep our eyes on everyone still on the list," Alyson suggested.

"You got any more of these cookies?" Trevor asked as he finished off the last one and poured himself a third glass of milk.

"Tons. In fact, I'll put some in a bag and you can take them home. My mom seems to be channeling Betty Crocker even more than usual. I think baking helps her deal with the stress of the carnival. I sure hope we can figure this out, and soon. It'd be a shame for everyone to go to so much trouble and not make enough to save the cemetery."

Chapter 7

On Friday morning they headed over to the town clerk's office only to discover that he had never been provided with a company bio. After discerning that the clerk had no other useful information to share, they went back to the mayor's office, only to be informed by his secretary that he was out of town and wouldn't be back until Monday morning.

"Why would the mayor go out of town on the opening weekend of the carnival?" Mac asked. "It's a big deal in this town; you'd think he'd want to be here."

"I guess he could have a family thing," Alyson suggested.

"Either that or he didn't want to be seen in public until he had the chance to get the red paint off his guilty hands," Trevor accused.

"Come on, Trev. Even if the mayor did paint your car, which I doubt, he'd only need a little turpentine to take care of the evidence." Mac dropped the empty soda can she had been holding into the trash can near the entrance to the rides and games. "This place is really hopping. Yesterday, when the trucks were just pulling up, I didn't think there would be any way they'd be ready for the opening tonight, but now we have a fully assembled tilt-a-whirl, a carousel, a twirling rocket, and a roller coaster. The other rides don't look too far behind."

"Yeah, and the game booths have been set up and stocked with prizes. I won a stuffed monkey for Stacy Keebler last year at the target shoot and got rewarded with all sorts of hugs and kisses," Trevor informed them. "I'm hoping for a repeat performance this year."

"Stacy Keebler moved to Florida," Mac reminded him.

"Oh, I'm totally fickle in my affections. Any pretty blonde will do."

"This looks like fun," Alyson commented as they continued to walk around, checking out the progress. "I'd love to try the roller coaster, and maybe the Ferris wheel. I've never been on a Ferris wheel."

"You've never been on a Ferris wheel before?" Trevor queried. "I got my first kiss sitting on top of the Ferris wheel in the second grade. Amy Lester. Now, she was a hot blonde. Seriously, if you've never tried it you've missed out on a lot."

"You kissed Amy Lester in the second grade?" Mac seemed surprised.

"More than once."

"Who are you and what did you do with my childhood friend who liked frogs and baseball? Not girls."

"You're a girl and you were my best friend."

"That's different. We didn't kiss."

"There's a lot you don't know, Mackster. I didn't tell you everything."

"Apparently not."

"So do they sell food here?" Alyson changed the subject.

"Yeah: corn dogs, hamburgers, popcorn, cotton candy, all sorts of good stuff," Mac answered. "The caramel corn is my favorite."

Alyson smiled as she watched the hustle and bustle created by the carnival crew. There was a sense of anticipation in the air as kids from around town came out to watch.

"I've been looking for you guys," Trevor's mom said as she walked up from behind them. She handed them each a piece of paper. "This is your schedule for the week. The Santa house opens tonight right after the tree lighting, so you'll need to be dressed and ready by five o'clock. Andy Meyer's group will relieve you at seven thirty. Your Santa shifts and play rehearsal schedule are both listed. There won't be any rehearsal over the weekend because the auditorium is being used for the children's pageant on Saturday and the holiday concert on Sunday. As for today, I could really use some help making sure all the carnival booths are well stocked with prizes. I've made a list of which booths should get which prizes."

"Oh, the target shoot has stuffed elephants this year," Trevor said as he perused the list after his mom headed off to find her next victim. "That ought to be good for a few smooches. How about you, Aly? You have a need for a stuffed elephant? They have four different colors."

"Thanks, but I'll win my own."

"How about you, Mac?"

"Not in a million years."

"You guys are no fun. I guess I'll have to see if Amy Lester is around."

"We'd better get started," Alyson said. "This is a pretty long list. It looks like lots of walking and carrying are in our future."

By the time they went home to shower and change into their Santa and elf costumes they were already exhausted. Everyone had agreed to bring a change of clothes so they could go to the carnival after their shift. Alyson threw a pair of jeans and a bright red sweater in her bag, then stopped to consider her reflection in the mirror. A year ago she wouldn't have been caught dead in this outfit. Oh, how the mighty had fallen. Pretty much everyone in her old high school would have a coronary if they could see her now. Popular, sophisticated Amanda Parker in a short red dress and green tights. Who'd have thought?

Tucker sat at her feet, wagging his tail. She knew he'd been missing her this week. She'd been too busy for many morning runs or afternoon romps. "Do you want to be a reindeer?"

Tucker barked once and thumped his tail at the sound of her voice. Alyson looked around her room. Trevor had bought her a pair of reindeer antlers at the Holiday Store when they were shopping for decorations. They were attached to a headband, but Alyson quickly modified them to tie around Tucker's head.

"There. You can be Dancer. Or would you prefer Dasher? Come on, we're going to be late."

Alyson picked up Trevor and Mac, then they headed downtown. The carnival area was already crowded by the time they arrived and people were parking a half mile away. Luckily, there were reserved parking spaces for the actors, so they were able to park near the Santa house. Alyson attached a leash to Tucker's collar and they all hurried to the entrance.

"Wow, half the state must be here," Alyson commented as they hurried inside and closed the door behind them.

"Yeah, opening weekend is always really big." Mac hung up her coat. "I'm sure we won't have a break at all once we start."

Alyson tied Tucker's leash to Santa's sleigh, then took off her own coat. Tucker curled up in the fake snow and watched the people around him.

By the time the doors to Santa's house opened exactly at five fifteen, the line had wound around more than once. Trevor was a natural Santa. In spite of his sometimes gruff exterior, he was gentle and friendly with the kids, patient as he listened to their lists and talked to them about their behavior over the past year. His smile seemed genuine when he handed each one a candy cane and wished them a Merry Christmas. Alyson had a new appreciation for this amazing person who had become her friend.

Mac's discomfort over her costume seemed to vanish once the kids came in. She greeted each one, calming the fears of the smallest ones and cracking jokes with the older ones.

Alyson was in charge of the camera. She took a picture of each child who sat on Santa's lap. Several kids wanted a picture with the doggie reindeer, and Tucker seemed to be in heaven from all the attention. At first Alyson hadn't been thrilled with her Santa assignment, but by the end of the shift, she was looking forward to the week ahead.

After they were finished they changed their clothes and headed over to the carnival. Alyson ordered herself a corn dog and an extra one for Tucker. Mac had nachos and Trevor a huge, sloppy chiliburger.

"I can't believe how much I'm enjoying this." Alyson dipped her batter-covered hot dog in mustard. "And Tucker loved the kids. I'm glad I brought him."

"After we eat we should check out the games," Trevor suggested. "The lines for the rides are a mile long."

"I'm in." Alyson nibbled on one of her garlic fries and looked around at the throngs of people hurrying every which way. "Although I bet the lines for the games are long too."

"The weekends are usually pretty crowded, but the weeknights aren't too bad," Mac informed her. "Of course, we have our shift at the Santa house, followed by rehearsal for the play all week. I hope my mom's not on the committee next year. It seems like the three of us got volunteered for more work than anyone else."

"Yeah, but it's for a good cause," Alyson reminded her. "If we can earn enough money we can save the old cemetery."

"I hope that with all the mishaps we aren't burning through our profits," Mac worried.

"We'll be fine. This place is rockin'. Let's go check it out."

They finished their food, then walked through the rides to the games. Children from one to ninety-one were having the time of their lives screaming on the roller coaster and getting dizzy on the tilt-a-whirl. As expected, the line for each ride was beyond long.

"Say, weren't you guys in the Santa house earlier?" the operator at the Ferris wheel asked as they paused to watch the fun.

"Yeah, that was us." Trevor nodded.

"You guys were great. My daughter was one of the kids who went through and she said you were the best Santa ever. The kid's quite a critic too. It was great of you to volunteer. Say, I have one last bucket open for this round. Want to take a ride? My treat. I think all three of you can fit in if you squeeze together."

"I have my dog." Alyson looked at Tucker.

"Oh, yeah. The reindeer. I'll keep an eye on him for you. He'll be fine."

"Want to?" Alyson asked the others.

"Sure, let's go for it." Trevor stepped into the bucket, followed by Mac. Alyson handed Tucker's leash to the operator, then squeezed in next to Mac. The man closed the door and started the ride.

"This is really a rush," Alyson breathed as they neared the top. "I can see the whole town."

Tucker barked as she rotated past him the first time around.

"It looks like the lines for the games are pretty long." Mac looked over the crowd from her vantage point. "We might need to wait until next week to try them out."

"Hey, look, there's Chelsea and Caleb in line for the tilt-a-whirl." Trevor leaned over the side of the bucket and pointed below.

"I can't believe they're dating." Mac leaned over Trevor to see down. "If there was ever a pair that didn't fit, it'd have to be them."

"I think it's pretty casual." Alyson leaned over her side of the bucket to look down. "Caleb said they're just friends. What was that?" She jumped at the sound of a loud pop as they neared the top their third time around.

"These rides are old and creaky. They make noises," Trevor reassured her. "I'm sure it's nothing."

"I don't know. It sure sounded like something." Alyson looked up toward the supports holding the bucket in place.

The machinery overhead groaned as the bucket swayed to and fro as they passed over the top of the wheel.

"It didn't sound like that before," Alyson insisted.

"Relax; I think we just have one or two revolutions left." Mac squeezed her hand.

As they passed the bottom for the third time, Tucker barked and the operator waved. Alyson relaxed as they started their fourth rotation. Surely they'd stop the ride if there was a problem.

Just as they reached the top, there was a loud twang as one of the supports gave way, and Alyson felt herself being thrown free of her seat.

She screamed as she was thrown into the air and reached out as she fell, grabbing on to the dangling door of the bucket. The support on the right side had come loose and the entire bucket was dangling from the left-side support.

"Hang on, Aly," Mac screamed from above her. "Don't let go."   '

Alyson looked up to see Mac and Trevor were still inside the bucket but hanging on for dear life themselves. The ride had stopped when the bucket broke free, but Alyson felt herself swaying as she dangled a hundred feet above the ground.

Trevor maneuvered himself to Mac's other side. Alyson clung to the side of the bucket with one hand and to Trevor's belt with the other. The bucket tipped further as he leaned over the side.

Alyson felt herself getting dizzy. Her arm burned and the fingers clinging to the door felt numb. She could hear Tucker barking frantically below her as the crowd screamed and scattered in panic.

"You need to reach up and grab my hand," Trevor commanded from above her.

"I can't."

"Yes, you can. You have to. Look at me."

Alyson looked up. Trevor was hanging over the side of the bucket as far as he could. His hand dangled near her head. She needed only to reach up with her other hand. Alyson summoned all her strength and reached for Trevor's hand. His grip felt like a vise as he slowly used his upper body strength to lift her to safety. Once she was inside the bucket, the operator slowly rotated the bucket toward the ground.

Alyson's nails dug into Trevor's arm as they were lowered to safety. By the time they reached the bottom, blood was trickling from her fingertips.

"Are you okay?" The Ferris wheel operator hurried over to them. "I don't know what happened. I checked everything over personally this morning. The bolts were tight, I swear."

Tucker pushed past the man as he threw himself across Alyson's legs. She was crying hysterically as she fell into his body.

"Can you walk?" Trevor asked from behind her. "We need to get out of here."

Alyson didn't say anything, just continued to cry as she stepped out of the broken bucket. As soon as he was free, Alyson wrapped her arms around Trevor's neck.

"Honey, I'm glad you're okay, but breathing is becoming an issue," he gasped.

Alyson let loose one of her arms, still holding on tight with the other as she pulled Mac into her embrace. The three friends stood hugging and crying as an emergency crew arrived.

After hours of being questioned by the police and poked and prodded by medical personnel, Alyson and the others were finally turned over to their terrified parents. The Ferris wheel operator was being questioned about the accident, as were the men who had set up the ride in the first place. It was closed indefinitely so a proper investigation could be conducted.

Tucker slept on Alyson's bed that night as she clung to his warmth. She tossed and turned as events from the evening haunted her dreams.

Chapter 8

By the time the morning rolled around, Tucker was glad to go out for his morning romp while Alyson staggered downstairs in search of coffee.

"I heard you moving around, so I made you some breakfast." Sarah set a plate with fluffy scrambled eggs, crisp bacon, and buttered toast in front of her. She filled a blue ceramic mug with coffee and set it next to a glass of freshly squeezed orange juice. "How are you feeling?"

Alyson took a long sip of coffee. "Okay; a little sore. I think every muscle in my body was yanked when I fell." She looked at the hand with which she had clung to life; it was cut and bruised. "I still feel a little shaky, but I guess I'll live."

"We've found replacements for your shifts in the Santa house tonight. I think you should stay in and rest."

"I'm not up for anything superphysical, but I'd like to see the guys. Maybe I'll call them to see if they want to hang out. Are you going to the carnival today?"

"I'm supposed to help with the children's pageant, but I'll call and have them find someone else if you want me to stay here."

"No, go ahead. I'll be fine."

Tucker scratched at the door to be let in. He came over and licked Alyson's hand before lying down at her feet. She petted her friend's head as she sipped her coffee, doubting she'd ever again look at a Ferris wheel with childlike enthusiasm. From now on, the merry-go-round would be her ride of choice.

After breakfast she called Mac and Trevor and arranged to have them come over later in the day. Something had happened last night—something more than an accident—and Alyson was determined to find out what it was.

Mac and Trevor arrived around noon carrying deli sandwiches, potato salad, and fresh-baked brownies from the sandwich shop.

"How are you feeling?" Mac asked Alyson as she picked at her potato salad.

"A little sore, but I'll be fine. How's your hand?" she asked Trevor. "Sorry for the puncture wounds."

"It's okay. I'm just glad I could reach you. I don't even want to think about what could have happened if someone else had been in our bucket. The green one in front of us had two little kids, and the red one behind us an older couple. If it had been either of them in the faulty bucket they would have fallen for sure."

"Doesn't it seem strange that it was our bucket that fell?" Mac asked. "I mean, first Trevor's car and now this. It's almost like we were targeted."

"Yeah, but there's no way the accident could have been planned. The attendant who offered us the ride couldn't have known when we'd be coming by or, for that matter, that we'd be coming by at all." Alyson repeatedly stabbed one of the potatoes in her salad as she spoke.

"Unless someone was watching us," Trevor said. "Maybe someone informed the operator that we were headed that way and he held the bucket open for us."

"There's no way he could have known when it would give way," Alyson argued. "Other people had been riding in that bucket all night."

"Unless they weren't," Mac theorized. "Maybe they'd been leaving it open until we came by."

"I guess." Alyson was still doubtful. "It would be easy enough to check out. But the operator didn't seem like the murderous type. He seemed genuinely shocked and horrified."

"I think we should ask around anyway," Mac said.

"Tomorrow," Trevor insisted. "Today we have a day off and I say we enjoy it. The rest of the week is bound to be busy."

"Agreed." Mac finished off her ham sandwich. "We could help Aly decorate her tree. It looks so lonely and naked. That is, unless you want to wait for your mom."

"No, I think she's so busy she won't mind at all. Besides, it isn't like it's one of our traditions." Alyson walked over to the hall closet and got out the decorations she'd bought. Trevor hung the lights while Alyson put on some Christmas music and Mac started a fire.

"So what are your Christmas traditions?" Mac asked as she worked.

"My parents usually had a huge open house on Christmas Eve, then we'd open presents on Christmas morning before going over to my grandparents' for a formal dinner. I'm not sure what we'll do this year, with just the two of us. Well, three with Tucker. How about you? What do you do?"

"Every Christmas Eve my aunts and uncles and cousins come over and we make a huge pot of spaghetti. The kids always get together and put on a play of some type for the adults. Afterward my dad reads 'The Night Before Christmas,' and my Uncle Joe reads the passage in the Bible about Jesus's birth. We sing some carols, exchange presents, and the adults share a couple of bottles of champagne. Like most of our holidays, it's loud and crowded and homey."

"Wow, that sounds so nice. I didn't have any cousins, so my Christmas celebrations were very grown-up. Christmas was usually just me and tons of adults, most of whom I barely knew. What about you, Trev? What do you do?"

"It depends. Sometimes everyone goes in different directions for the holiday and I go over to Mac's. If my family is in town we usually make a turkey and watch Christmas specials on TV. I like *A Charlie Brown Christmas* the best."

After the white lights were strung around the tree, Alyson helped Trevor hang the ornaments while Mac wound garlands around the banister and across the mantel.

"You could use some more ornaments for the tree," Trevor commented. "It's such a huge tree, it still looks a little bare."

"I guess we could go pick some up." Alyson shrugged.

"I have a better idea." Trevor put the empty boxes from the decorations back in the closet. "Bromwell Stables always offers sleigh rides downtown during the carnival. How about we pick up your decorations, then go for a sleigh ride and have dinner?"

"Sounds great, but I see one problem with your idea," Alyson said. "There's no snow. How are we going to take a sleigh ride without any snow?"

"The sleighs are actually on wheels, but the effect's the same. Trust me, you'll love it. They do a grand tour through the town, focusing on the areas that are decorated the best."

"I'm in. How about you, Mac?"

"I'll need to stop at home and change if we're going to go out for dinner. I don't think overalls and a Grinch sweatshirt is really appropriate attire."

Alyson quickly changed her clothes, being sure to dress warmly for the sleigh ride. She called her mom to fill her in on their plans, then they headed over to Mac's and Trevor's so they could change too.

The sleigh ride was everything Trevor had promised and more. A huge Clydesdale pulled each sleigh, which was driven by a man wearing an authentic eighteenth-century costume. Trevor sat between Mac and Alyson with his arms around each of them in an attempt to offer body warmth.

The sleigh took them through downtown, with its bright lights, decorated store windows, huge Christmas tree, and ice-skating pond. It traveled past the perimeter of the carnival, then wound its way into several neighborhoods, where the residents had gone all out with holiday decorations.

Alyson and Mac each rested their head on Trevor's shoulder as they glided smoothly through the Christmas fairyland.

"I wish it would snow." Mac sighed. "It's certainly cold enough."

Alyson looked up into the star-filled sky. "I doubt snow is in our future, but look at the stars; they're so bright. I love the winter sky here. Without all the lights from the city everything looks so close. Look at that one bright star." Alyson pointed in the distance. "It's so much more brilliant than the others."

"It's the Christmas star," Trevor informed her.

"Really? Are you sure?"

"Well, no. But it's Christmas time and it's by far the largest, most radiant star in the sky."

"It's beautiful. Almost magical. Maybe we should make a wish. 'Twinkle, twinkle, little star ...'" Alyson began.

"Actually, I'm pretty sure what we're looking at is a planet, not a star," Mac pointed out, "but I'm all for making a wish anyway. We could use a little magic this Christmas season."

When the hour-long ride ended, they tipped their driver, then headed over to the restaurant for dinner. The seaside village, built on the old wharf, went all out with their decorations. There were thousands of white twinkle lights strung along the roofs of all the buildings. The bushes and trees in front of the businesses that lined the wooden pier were brightly lit as well. Someone had set up a life-size Santa's village, complete with mechanical reindeer and a jolly old Santa in a sleigh in the center of the shopping center. At the end of the wharf sat the restaurant where they had their reservation.

Inside, the restaurant was a bit more elegant, with several artificial trees decorated with white lights and gold and silver ornaments. There was a crackling fire in the stone fireplace and soft Christmas jazz played in the background.

The host showed them to a table by the window. The moon reflected brightly off the gently rolling waves below. The table was set with a white lace tablecloth over a dark red underlay. A merrily flickering candle sat in the center of the beautifully set table, surrounded by freshly cut pine boughs. After handing each of them a menu the host promised that a waiter would be by shortly.

"Everything looks so good. I have no idea what to order." Alyson perused the varied offerings.

"The scampi is great," Trevor offered. "And the fresh fish of the day is usually good. I think I'll have the seafood lasagna, though."

"How about you, Mac?"

"I think I'll wait to hear the specials before I decide. Sometimes they have a really unique way of preparing the fresh fish they catch each day. Say, isn't that Chelsea with Tony Sanders just coming in? I thought she was dating Caleb. Oh, great; she sees us and is heading our way."

Chelsea rushed over to hug Trevor while her date waited near the hostess stand. "I heard you almost died. I've been frantic with worry. I've been calling your house all day. Where have you been?"

"Hanging out with Mac and Alyson."

"With your trauma? Shouldn't you have been home resting up?"

"I'm fine; besides, it was Alyson who almost died, not me."

"Well, I'm just glad you're okay."

Chelsea sat down in the empty fourth chair next to Trevor. "I've been going crazy since I heard it was you in that death trap last night. And it isn't just me. Everyone in town is totally freaking out. They even had an emergency town council meeting today, even though the mayor is totally AWOL."

"AWOL?" Alyson asked. She knew the mayor was out of town but she hoped Chelsea would have additional information considering her father was on the council.

"He left town unexpectedly and didn't tell anyone where he was going. People on the town council have tried to call him on his cell like a million times, but he hasn't answered."

"Did anyone check with his wife?" Alyson asked.

"He doesn't have one. He was caught boinking Mrs. Farrell last year and his wife booted him. I hear she's taking him for everything he's got in the divorce."

"So why did the town council meet?" Alyson asked.

"Because the investigation into the incident on the Ferris wheel showed that it definitely wasn't an accident. Someone tampered with the locking mechanism. And that's not even the worst part."

"What's the worst part?" Mac was sitting on the edge of her seat.

"Mrs. Conway, the mayor's secretary, never came home from work last night. They found her car abandoned on the highway. They think maybe whoever sabotaged the Ferris wheel might have offed her."

"God, I hope not," Alyson breathed.

"The Ferris wheel operator remembered seeing the mayor arguing with someone on Thursday, before he left town. Then he disappeared on Friday and his secretary never made it home. Some people think they both might be dead. Of course, there are others who think the mayor and his secretary simply took off on a clandestine weekend away. Everyone knows the mayor has had more lovers than a bitch in heat."

"What are they doing to find the mayor?" Trevor asked.

"The normal stuff. They put out an APB on his car and are tracking his cell phone. The cops are on top of it; I just hope they don't find another fresh grave in the cemetery."

"Has anyone thought about canceling the carnival?" Alyson asked. "It'd be horrible if there was another accident."

"It was discussed, but they decided to just step up security instead. They have people watching the rides twenty-four hours a day, and there'll be inspections every morning. I'm not planning to go on any more rides. I mean, that could have been me last night. I wanted to go on the Ferris wheel, but Caleb wanted to ride the tilt-a-whirl first. It's like he doesn't even know you're supposed to do what the girl wants on a date. But his total lack of proper dating etiquette could have saved my life. I can't even begin to tell you how totally scared I was when I heard all the commotion coming from the Ferris wheel. Well, I'd better go. Tony looks like he's going to have an aneurysm. I swear, guys can be so possessive sometimes." Chelsea kissed Trevor full on the lips. "Be careful, okay?"

"Wow. I hope the mayor and Mrs. Conway are okay." Alyson watched Chelsea saunter away. "It sounds like whoever we're dealing with is really dangerous. The question is, if the incidents are tied to the sale of the cemetery why would any company care enough about that particular piece of land to resort to violence? Maybe our theory about everything that's happened being tied to the sale is wrong."

"Maybe, but I say we step up our investigation into the company," Mac said. "I smell a fox in the hen house. Something just doesn't add up."

Chapter 9

They had the first shift at the Santa house the next day. After a restless night filled with disturbing thoughts, it was a sleepy-eyed group that met a little before noon.

"Those kids out there are expecting to see *jolly* old Saint Nick and his *merry* elves," Alyson reminded them as they all nursed cups of coffee. "We're going to have to dig deep to give them what they want. We can slip into nice, peaceful comas after our shift."

"I don't think I slept at all." Mac yawned. "I couldn't stop thinking about poor Mrs. Conway."

"I know what you mean." Trevor tapped the bottom of his upturned cup to get the last drop of caffeine.

Alyson looked out from the window of the house at the long line of hyper children. Christmas carols played over the loudspeakers as harried adults glanced at their watches in anticipation of the noon opening.

Mac unlocked the door, Alyson checked to make sure the camera was focused, and Trevor pulled his beard into place. "Smiles, everyone," Mac reminded them as the first toddlers began funneling through.

Once they got started everyone seemed to wake up. The enthusiasm of the children was infectious. Most of the older children asked for video games and electronic equipment, while the younger ones wanted the more traditional dolls and action figures. Bikes and skateboards were popular items, as were board games and sporting goods. One little boy even asked for a pair of socks.

Alyson saw that Trevor seemed to be enjoying his job just as much as he had on the first day, talking and joking with each kid. Even though the shaggy beard concealed his face, she could see his smile was genuine, as evidenced by the twinkle in his eyes. She'd paused to change the memory card in her digital camera when she noticed Trevor trying to coax a Christmas wish from a withdrawn little girl. Finally, the girl leaned forward and whispered into his ear. Alyson clicked the picture just as Trevor's jaw dropped.

"That's a pretty big wish," Trevor said, and the girl's eyes grew teary. "But I'll see what I can do."

The girl hugged him, then got off his lap and ran toward the exit without waiting to get the claim slip for her complimentary photo. Alyson looked around, but she was gone, and there didn't seem to have been an adult accompanying her.

Alyson looked back toward Trevor as a toddler was placed in his lap. He smiled as he spoke to her, but the merriment in his eyes had been replaced with anxiety and concern. They had another hour until their shift was over. Alyson made eye contact with him, trying to convey her support.

"What happened back there?" Alyson asked him as soon as the next team showed up to relieve them. "The little girl with the long blond braids. What'd she ask for?"

"She said, 'The bad man has my mommy. Can you find her and bring her home?' I was speechless. I didn't know what to do."

"So you told her you'd try. Oh, Trev, do you think she's Mrs. Conway's daughter?"

"I don't know for sure. We need to find out."

"I have the claim slip for the photo I took. She ran off without it and I stuck it in my pocket. Let's get the picture and ask around."

Alyson took the slip of paper from her pocket and walked back into the Santa house just as Mac was walking out.

"Hey, what's up?" Mac asked. "I thought you were going to change."

"I am, I just need to get something first. Trevor's right outside; he'll fill you in. I'll join you in a minute."

After they'd changed into their street clothes, they went in search of someone who might recognize the girl in the photo.

"Yes, that's Mindy Conway," Mrs. Stein, one of Cutter's Cove's first-grade teachers confirmed. "She's a quiet little thing. I had her in my class last year. Why are you looking for her anyway?"

"She forgot her picture," Alyson improvised. "We wanted to get it to her if she's still around."

"Well, that's mighty nice of you. I think I saw her with some other kids over by the merry-go-round."

"Thanks; we'll check."

Alyson, Mac, and Trevor walked toward the carnival, which was in full swing. The Ferris wheel was still closed, but all the other rides were crowded with screaming, laughing kids of all ages.

"I don't see her." Trevor paused near the merry-go-round, scanning the area.

"She could be long gone by now," Mac said. "Hey, isn't that guy running the tilt-a-whirl the same one who was operating the Ferris wheel the other night?"

"Yeah, I think so." Alyson nodded.

"I'm surprised to see him here after what happened."

"He said he didn't do anything to cause the accident. I guess his story checked out," Alyson surmised.

"Maybe, but I'd still like the opportunity to question him myself." Mac glared in his direction.

"Why don't we just ask him if he'd mind answering some questions?" Trevor suggested. "Come on."

They headed toward the tilt-a-whirl and asked the man if he had a few minutes to chat.

"Sure, I'd be happy to; just give me a minute to get someone to cover for me." The man flagged down someone who just happened to be passing by. The guy must have agreed to cover for him because the Ferris wheel operator headed toward them a moment later.

"I'm real sorry about everything," he apologized. "I can't imagine what happened. I checked everything over after the crew finished setting up. I swear, everything was tightened down real good."

"Did you see anyone near the Ferris wheel who may have been tampering with it after you checked it?" Mac asked.

"Not a soul. Of course, we finished setting up on Thursday and didn't start operating until Friday night, so I guess someone could have tampered with it in the meantime."

"You travel all over the country with this equipment. Has anything like this ever happened before?" Trevor asked.

He shook his head. "We're real careful. Safety is number one with our company."

"Have you noticed anything suspicious at all?" Alyson asked. "Maybe someone lurking around who shouldn't be there?"

The man thought a minute. "Not really. A lot of people come by here, though, so it's hard to say. I did see a man having a heated argument with a man on Thursday evening. I remember thinking at the time that it was odd they'd be having such a serious discussion in such a public place. I asked one of the locals we'd hired to help with the setup who the men were. He told me one of the men was the mayor of Cutter's Cove, but he didn't know who the other guy was."

"Did you hear what they were arguing about?" Mac asked.

"I try not to eavesdrop." He paused.

"Do you remember what the guy the mayor was arguing with looked like?" Trevor asked.

"'Bout six feet tall, dark hair."

"Anything else?" Trevor asked.

"He had a huge diamond ring on his left hand. I noticed it because the sun reflected off it."

"Is anything being done to make sure there isn't another accident?" Alyson asked. "If someone is tampering with the rides I'd hate to see someone else get hurt."

"We're doing a thorough inspection of every piece of equipment before the carnival opens each day," he said, confirming what Chelsea had told them the night before. "And we've added twenty-four-hour security. Don't you worry your pretty little head. These rides are safe as houses."

"Okay, well, thanks for taking the time to answer our questions. If you think of anything else we'll be in the Santa house in the afternoons all week."

"You kids take care now." The man walked back toward the tilt-a-whirl.

"What now?" Mac asked.

"I told a pretty little girl I'd try to bring her mommy home and that's what I intend to do," Trevor declared. "I say we get into serious research mode. We need a plan and a computer. We'll stop by Mac's and get her laptop, then head over to Alyson's."

"Sounds like a plan," Alyson agreed. "I'll just stop by the auditorium to tell my mom we're leaving. She's helping out with the concert today."

Alyson reached her house before the others. She let Tucker out for a romp, then built a fire, turned on the lights on the tree, and put a Christmas CD in the player. Rummaging in the kitchen, she threw together a plate of cold cuts, fruit, and cheese and put a pot of hot cider on the stove to simmer. She was lighting the red holly berry candles on the mantel when the others arrived.

Mac plugged her computer into an empty outlet, then set up shop on the coffee table in front of the crackling fire. Trevor helped Alyson carry the food into the living room, then they all got to work.

"We're going to have a hard time finding much more than we already have," Mac commented as she typed rapidly. "Without any new information from the mayor we're pretty much back where we were on Thursday evening. Oh, hey, that's new."

"What'd you find?" Trevor asked.

"Controlling interest in Psycorp is owned by an Ian Wall. Wall also holds a majority interest in another company, Chemlab, in Portland."

"Chemlab?" Alyson asked.

"They produce things like fertilizers and pesticides for farmers. They've been around quite a while and it appears they're fairly profitable."

"So why create a new company if you already have a successful one in this area?" Trevor asked.

"Maybe the new company is going to produce or manufacture something else," Alyson guessed. "Conglomerates do that all the time. They may have one company to manufacture and distribute soft drinks and another to distribute snack foods."

"True, but if they had an established business in Portland why wouldn't that have been brought up at the town council meeting?" Trevor asked. "And why mislead everyone about some vague East Coast presence if they're really based right here in Oregon?"

"Both good questions. You find anything else, Mac?" Alyson wondered.

"Not yet, but I'll keep looking. There's a lot more information available about Chemlab. Although, like Psycorp, they're not publicly traded, there's financial information, credit reports, that sort of thing. Oh, hey, wait a minute. Look at that."

"What?" Alyson and Trevor both asked.

"Chemlab was under investigation last year for suspicion of mishandling toxic waste. Nothing was ever proven, so no legal action was taken, but it says here that if proof had been found the owner and plant manager would both have gone to prison."

"Suddenly we have a reason for the new company and the misinformation with the whole East Coast thing." Trevor walked across the room and started to read the screen over Mac's shoulder. "Even though nothing was ever proven, people in this area probably were aware of the scandal. I doubt an offer by Chemlab to buy the old cemetery would be seriously considered, but an offer by Psycorp, an unknown company, might be."

"Okay, so Chemlab wants to buy the old cemetery, so they create a brand-new, scandal-free company to be the front. Why?" Alyson asked. "They have a huge plant outside of Portland, they already have most of the business in the area, why would they want a piece of land in Cutter's Cove? And, more important, what do they plan to do with it?"

"That I don't know. Mac, any ideas?" Trevor asked.

"It doesn't make sense, unless, as Alyson brought up before, they want to branch off into another type of business and want a separate plant to do it. But why here?"

"And, more importantly, how does this piece of information help us with the missing mayor and secretary or the mishaps at the carnival?" Trevor added. "We have all these events that all seem suspicious, but how do they fit together? Or do they fit together at all? Maybe the Chemlab cover-up has nothing to do with the missing people or the sabotage at the carnival. I guess we should consider the fact that we might have a bunch of completely unrelated events."

Alyson picked up the pad she had set on the table in front of her and considered the notes she'd been jotting down. "Okay, what do we know? We have the list of suspects we created on Thursday. As of then we'd narrowed things down to the mayor, Mr. Green, Dr. Went, Mrs. Conway, the town clerk, and the bookkeeper."

"Actually, I think we should eliminate the two town council members if we take the attack on Raquel into account. They wouldn't have known about our visit to the mayor," Mac suggested.

"Honestly, as far as the sabotage of the carnival is concerned, my money is on the mayor. He had opportunity and motive," Trevor pointed out.

"He also must have known the truth about Chemlab," Mac surmised. "I can't believe he would have presented Psycorp's offer to buy the land if he hadn't checked them out first."

"Yeah, but he's an elected official," Alyson said. "Why would he cover up for Psycorp? He really has nothing to gain except a balanced budget if the sale goes through. While I realize that would make his life easier, I wonder if it would be worth the fallout if someone realized he'd been part of a cover-up."

Alyson doodled on her pad as she thought. "The mayor's secretary and the town clerk both had access to all the information needed to sabotage the carnival. Maybe we should reconsider our original theory that Psycorp is bribing someone. The secretary and town clerk certainly had less to lose than the mayor if they were found out."

"Yeah, except that the secretary is missing along with the mayor," Trevor pointed out.

"Maybe the town clerk kidnapped them both. Or maybe not," Mac countered as Alyson and Trevor responded with doubt-filled expressions. "This whole thing is really confusing. On one hand, everything seems to fit into one big conspiracy. On the other, nothing really fits at all."

"The only thing we can say for certain is that the mayor seems to be the common link between all the individual events," Alyson concluded. "He had access to all aspects of the carnival, he must have known about the Psycorp cover-up, and he's one of two missing persons. The Ferris wheel operator also put him at that scene under suspicious circumstances. I think we all know there's only one thing to do: We have to break into the mayor's office and go through his files."

"Are you sure?" Mac gasped. "There must be a better way. I mean, I agree we need to find out what the mayor knows, but I really don't like the idea of spending the next ten to twenty in the pen."

"How else are we going to get a look at his files?" Alyson asked. "I doubt anyone is just going to let us in, especially with all the hoopla that's going on over his disappearance. We need to break in and we need to do it soon. Tonight."

"Tonight?" Mac groaned. "But *A Charlie Brown Christmas* is on tonight. We were going to watch it. Remember?"

"I know, but we'll have to record it. It has to be tonight. If the mayor doesn't show up for work tomorrow as scheduled there's definitely going to be an investigation."

"But Snoopy…"

"Come on, Mac," Trevor encouraged her. "I know you're scared, but Aly's right. Now is our best shot at getting a look at the mayor's files before the cops start snooping through everything."

"Okay, but orange isn't my best color, so we'd better not get caught."

"We'll have to wait until the carnival is over for the night," Alyson realized. "There are way too many people downtown right now."

"The rides close down at seven o'clock tonight," Trevor reminded her, "on account of the concert in the auditorium. I say we do it then. Everyone will be inside listening to the music, and if someone does see us lurking around, we can come up with a better excuse for being in the area than we would be at midnight."

"Agreed. We'll do it then. Does anyone know how to pick a lock?" Alyson asked.

"Oh, sure, 'cause I'm such a big thief," Mac answered sarcastically.

"Come on, Mac; we all need to work together." Trevor put his arm around her shoulders. "We need to get into the mayor's office and we need to do it quietly. I doubt there will be any open windows with the weather this cold, so we'll have to go in through the front door, which is sure to be locked. Maybe we should just ask someone for a key."

"Like who?" Alyson asked doubtfully.

"That I don't know. Come on, let's put our thinking caps on. We've been there all week, helping out, working the Santa house. There must be some excuse we can come up with for why someone who has a key will believe we need to use it. Think, people."

"Okay, who has the key?" Mac asked.

"The mayor, who's missing. His secretary, who's also missing," Alyson started. "Who else is there?"

"The janitor," Mac declared.

"Of course. Do you think he'll be around on a Sunday evening?" Alyson asked.

"With all the stuff that's going on, someone from maintenance will have to be there."

"Okay, so what excuse do we offer to get the janitor to lend us his key?" Trevor asked.

They sat in silence for several minutes. Alyson doodled on her notepad. Mac drummed her nails on the keyboard of her laptop. Trevor paced back and forth. Christmas carols played in the background, the fire danced, and the candles flickered.

"I haven't got a thing," Trevor concluded.

"Me neither," Mac said.

"We could say we left something in the office," Alyson suggested weakly.

"Like what? I mean, why would we even have been in there to leave something?" Mac asked.

"Well, at least I came up with something," Alyson defended herself.

"Wait a minute." Mac sat forward. "The janitor must have a master key that fits all the locks. I mean, there are dozens of town offices and facilities. We don't need to ask for a key to the mayor's office; we only need to get hold of the master for a few minutes. We can unlock the door, then return the key before he suspects anything."

"That could work." Trevor nodded. "We could say we need to photocopy something for the Christmas concert, so we need to get into town hall to use the photocopier."

"What's to keep the janitor from just coming with us and opening the main door?" Mac asked. "There's a photocopier in the secretary's office."

Trevor laid out a plan. "We'll need a distraction. One of us will cause it. Then someone else will ask for the key to an office with a photocopier. The third will keep watch. The one with the key will open the door, go inside, and start looking around while someone else returns the key to the janitor. Then that person will come back to the office to help look around while the third person keeps the janitor busy."

"Huh?" Mac asked.

"Look, Mac, I know you're not comfortable with breaking into the mayor's office, so you'll be distraction girl while Aly and I do the deed. Just keep him busy until the two of us get back."

"How do I do that?"

"Oh, oh, I have a plan," Alyson said excitedly. "We're going to need something absorbent."

"Mr. Brownly, Mr. Brownly." Mac ran toward the janitor, who was setting up folding chairs in the church auditorium later that evening. "Come quick. The toilets are overflowing and flooding the bathrooms and the hallway."

"Which toilets?" Mr. Brownly ran toward the janitor's closet for a mop and a bucket.

"All of them. We need to hurry; people are already lining up for the concert. We can't let them in; the whole hallway's flooded."

Mr. Brownly grabbed the mop and bucket, and a plunger and toolkit, and hurried toward the hastily arranged diversion. Mac followed along behind, giving a big thumbs-up to Alyson, who was waiting near the kitchen door.

"My gosh, what could have happened?" Mr. Brownly surveyed the mess caused by six overflowing toilets, three in the women's restroom and three in the men's.

"I have no idea," Mac said innocently. "I just came over to wash my hands and found standing water in the hallway. I immediately ran to get you."

"It's a good thing you did. If we hadn't seen this before letting in the crowd, we would have had an even bigger mess."

"Mr. Brownly." Alyson hurried up with a concert program in her hand. "You have to let me into town hall. I need to use the copier right away. Someone messed up the programs and the order in which the performers come on is all wrong. I need to print new agendas for the performers or nothing will match."

"I can't leave right now; I have a bit of a mess on my hands. Here, just take the key, but be sure to bring it right back once you open the door. That key goes to all the town offices, so don't lose it."

"I won't. I'll be back in a jiffy. Thanks."

Alyson let Trevor and herself into town hall. She unlocked the mayor's office, and while she made twenty-five unnecessary copies of the program, Trevor slipped into the inner office and pulled the door closed behind him. Alyson hurried back to the janitor carrying the copies and handed him back the key. After making sure she hadn't been observed, she slipped back through the door she had kept ajar with a stick and joined Trevor in the mayor's chamber.

"What are we looking for exactly?" Trevor asked her.

"I'm not sure. Anything that might give us more information about what's going on with Psycorp, and what the mayor might know about it."

Alyson picked up a folder marked *Christmas Carnival*. There was information inside concerning all aspects of the carnival, including the contract with the company that provided the rides, the lease agreement for the storage unit where the sets for the play were stored, a copy of the invoice from the wholesale market where the ingredients for the Christmas candy had been ordered, and a copy of the ad that was to have been placed in the Portland newspaper.

"The mayor definitely had all the information needed to be our saboteur," Alyson concluded. "There's even a list in the back of this folder with pageant sets, grocery supplies, and decorations checked off. Everything that's gone wrong except the graffiti on Raquel and the sabotage to the ride is covered."

"Maybe someone else is responsible for those two things," Trevor suggested.

"Oh, great, two suspects. We're having a hard enough time nailing down the one. If the mayor is responsible for the first group of mishaps, who's responsible for the last two?"

Trevor shrugged. "Maybe it was the mayor, but maybe they were spontaneous rather than planned."

"Maybe. Let's look around some more, then get out of here. Eventually, Mr. Brownly is going to come by to make sure we locked up properly. Mac did a great job creating a sense of panic, but she won't be able to keep it up forever."

Alyson picked up the mayor's messages and began rummaging through them. There were several from the same person, a Carl Reinhart from Chemlab. The last one had been left on the previous Thursday at three o'clock in the afternoon. Whoever took the message—probably his secretary—had written down his name, business affiliation, phone number, and the words *arrives at four*.

"Check this out." Alyson held up the message. "The Ferris wheel operator said he saw the mayor arguing with someone late Thursday afternoon. Did he happen to say what time that was?"

"Not that I recall."

"I wonder if the visitor from Chemlab is the quarrelsome stranger. We need to go back to ask him the approximate time he witnessed that exchange. If the mayor and his Chemlab partner in crime came to a parting of the minds, maybe there's a link to the argument and the mayor's disappearance."

"I don't get the possible connection."

"We need to assume someone from Chemlab and the mayor are working together to make sure the carnival isn't a success so the town council will have no option but to approve the sale of the land to Psycorp. Something happened and the two disagreed on how to proceed. Maybe the guy from Chemlab realized the mayor knew too much and was a danger to the plan, so he offed him, or maybe just kidnapped him."

"I don't know, Aly; kidnap or murder over the sale of a piece of real estate? Seems a bit severe. There are tons of other parcels where Chemlab could build a manufacturing plant if that one didn't work out."

"True."

"Besides, I still don't get the mayor's role in this. Why would he even get involved in something that could hurt the town and ruin his own reputation?"

"I don't know; it was just a theory. Let's check out the secretary's desk, then get out of here."

Alyson and Trevor opened file cabinets and thumbed through folders, looking for anything that might link all these seemingly random events together. There were more files than they dared take time to look through, so they focused their attention on the ones on top of the desk. One file in particular stood out. It appeared to be filled with financial records for the town of Cutter's Cove. There were financial statements, budgets, and bank statements among other reports concerning annual projections and cost analyses. Alyson was just about to return the folder to the desk when something caught her eye. Removing several sheets of paper, she squinted as she tried to understand what she was looking at.

"I think I found something. Maybe even our proof."

"Whatcha got?"

"I'll need more time to sort this all out, but it looks like there are some discrepancies in the financial records for the town. There are a number of withdrawals circled on the statements. They're all for between two and five thousand dollars in even amounts. See, here's one for five thousand dollars in October and another one for three thousand in November. It looks like these statements go back about a year. Someone must have questioned the withdrawals; there are red question marks on the affected statements."

"Maybe someone's pocketing town funds."

"Maybe."

"The mayor?"

"There's no way to know for sure. Maybe we should photocopy these and show them to Mac."

"We'd better hurry. Who knows how long ..." Trevor stopped to listen. "What was that?" Tiptoeing quietly over to the door to the outer reception area, he cracked it open and peeked out. "Oh, crap. The janitor is headed down the hall."

"Quick, go back in the mayor's office and close the door. Quietly! We should hide behind the desk in case he looks in."

Trevor and Alyson crouched down low behind the desk, hoping Mr. Brownly wouldn't come into the inner office. The janitor could be heard doing something in the outer office as the minutes ticked slowly by. Alyson tried to steady her breathing as they waited. Trevor sat cross-legged, resting his elbows on his knees. He massaged his forehead with his fingertips as the time crept by. After what seemed like an eternity, the man opened the door to the mayor's office. Alyson put her hand over her mouth to keep from gasping as he started to walk toward the desk. Alyson was sure he could hear the deafening sound of the beating of her heart. He was leaning over to pick up the trash can at the side of the desk, a move that was sure to expose them, when the cell phone attached to his belt rang.

"Not again. I'll be right there," he barked into it. "Damn toilets." He turned around and walked back through the door, closing it behind him.

"Thank you, Mac," Alyson whispered as she heard the front door close. She took a deep breath and tried to stand on still shaking legs. "Let's get out of here before he comes back." She slipped the file of financial information under her coat and crept toward the front door. Opening it slowly, the pair left the office.

"That was close." Trevor breathed a sigh of relief as they jogged over to the auditorium to find Mac.

"Tell me about it. My heart hasn't stopped pounding yet."

They snuck in the back door to the auditorium, where the concert was in full swing. A group from the elementary school, dressed all in red and green, sang a merry rendition of "Rudolph the Red-Nosed Reindeer." The giant tree in the corner was decorated with hundreds of tiny white lights and shiny red balls. Streamers of garland and tiny twinkle lights were strung everywhere, giving the auditorium a magical feel. The festive coziness seemed lost on Mac, however, who was pacing near the hallway leading to the bathrooms.

"What took you so long? I have no idea what I was going to do if you hadn't shown up. There's no way the janitor was going to believe the toilets just happened to clog up three times in one night. Did you find anything?"

"Yeah, but I don't want to talk about it here," Alyson whispered. "Let's go to my house and we'll see if we can decipher the information in the file I stole."

"You stole a file!" Mac screeched a little too loudly. "I mean, you stole a file?" she whispered. "What if someone finds out?"

"Don't worry; we'll put it back after we have a chance to look through it."

"You mean we're going to have to break in again? My mom's going to have a cow when I'm put in jail. Especially right before Christmas."

"You're not going to be arrested. I'll slip in and leave the file on the secretary's desk tomorrow. It's a regular business day. I'm sure the door will be open."

"Not if the mayor and Mrs. Conway are both still missing."

"We'll cross that bridge when we get to it. Come on, let's get out of here."

Alyson spread out the contents of the stolen file on the kitchen table as soon as they reassembled at her house. She threw a log on the fire she had built in the old brick fireplace as Mac looked through the pages of financial information.

"You said you found this folder on the secretary's desk?" Mac sorted the paperwork into several different piles.

"Yeah." Alyson set a plate of cheese and fruit on the table next to the crusty bread her mom had picked up from the bakery earlier in the day.

"You got any butter for the bread?" Trevor asked as he bit into one of the cheese wedges. "Olives would be good too, if you have any. Green ones."

Alyson sorted through the refrigerator for the requested items. "How about you, Mac; any special requests?"

"No, I'm good."

"So can you make anything out of this stuff?" Alyson sat down next to Mac and waited for her to finish reading.

"We're going to need to do some more research to know for sure, but I can see several different possibilities. The most logical one is that the bookkeeper could have had a question about the withdrawals and given the folder to the mayor's secretary so she could look into them. Following that scenario the expenditures might even turn out to be legit. In fact, I think we should consider the very real possibility that there's nothing sinister going on here and we just committed a felony for nothing."

"I doubt stealing a folder is a felony," Alyson countered. "Besides, what about all the other stuff that's been going on? If someone was embezzling money, maybe everything else that's happened is part of a cover-up."

Mac popped a grape into her mouth. "Maybe. If there's someone embezzling money I see three possible suspects. The mayor could be the guilty party and the bookkeeper might have found out and brought the statements to the secretary. That would explain why they were on her desk."

"Or," Trevor interrupted, "maybe the secretary was the embezzler and the bookkeeper found out and confronted her."

"That was one of my theories," Mac responded. "Let me finish."

"Okay, sorry."

"The third possibility is that the bookkeeper is embezzling money and the mayor noticed the discrepancy and asked the secretary to look into it."

"How do we figure out who the guilty party is?" Trevor asked. "Whoever's stealing the money is probably the same degenerate who defiled my Raquel. Someone's gonna pay for what they did."

"Can we figure out where the money went?" Alyson asked.

"The easiest way to do that would be to get a look at the bookkeeper's trial balance for each of the affected months. Theoretically, in order for the check ledgers to balance with the financial statements, the withdrawal would have had to be coded to a specific account. That might give us an idea of where the money went. Of course, if the withdrawal is coded to something vague, like miscellaneous expenses, it really won't tell us anything."

"Are the withdrawals in the form of cashed checks or teller withdrawals?" Alyson asked.

"Neither, actually, at least for the most recent months. It looks like the money was simply transferred to another account."

"So whose account was it transferred into?" Trevor leaned over Mac's shoulder. "Whoever got the money is the thief."

"I'm not sure. I would like to point out, though, that the withdrawals could still be legit. People pay bills online all the time. What we might be seeing is simply the electronic bill that someone circled because they questioned the usage."

"Okay," Alyson leaned forward onto her elbows, "so it sounds like we need to get hold of the trial balances. If the withdrawals are okay they should show up as a legitimate expense. If they're stashed somewhere hokey, like a miscellaneous account, we research further."

"So how do we get a look at the trial balances?" Mac asked.

"We're going to need another diversion."

"I was afraid you were going to say that."

Chapter 10

"You kids are here early," Trevor's mom said the next morning. "I wasn't expecting to see you until later this afternoon."

"There was a little girl in the Santa house yesterday who was a diabetic and couldn't take one of the candy canes. We thought it would be a good idea to have some sugarless candy as an alternative," Trevor explained. "We weren't busy this morning so we thought we'd go pick some up."

"That's a wonderful idea. I'll call over to the bookkeeper to have her give you some money from petty cash. Just be sure to give her the receipt and any change you have by the end of the day. She's a real stickler for keeping the books straight."

"No problem," Trevor agreed. "We'll head over right now. We want to catch her before she heads out to lunch."

"You've got time. She goes to lunch from noon to one thirty every day. She told me she takes a spinning class over at the Y, so her hours are pretty regular."

"That's good to know, but I think we'll head over now anyway. We planned to have an early lunch somewhere ourselves," Trevor explained.

They headed over to the bookkeeper's office.

"That tidbit about the spinning class was a helpful piece of intel," Mac commented. "Now we don't have to wait around watching for her to leave. We'll just come back by a little after noon."

"Okay; you guys keep her talking and I'll slip some tape over the door latch," Alyson instructed.

"Don't you think she'll notice the tape?" Mac worried.

"No. She won't be looking for it. She'll probably just pull the door closed behind her and never notice."

"Good morning, Mrs. Cranston," Trevor said to the bookkeeper. "Did my mom call over to let you know we'd be coming by for some petty cash?"

"She did. I think your idea to get some sugarless candy is wonderful. My niece is diabetic. I'll be sure to send her over this week. She always feels left out when her siblings get a candy cane and she has to pass." She handed them the money. "Just bring me back the change and the receipt. I'll be out to lunch until one thirty, but any time before five is okay."

"Wow, she was really nice," Mac observed. "I hope she's not the bad guy. I feel a little bad about even sneaking into her office."

"Don't worry, Mac. She'll never know we were there. We'll get in, look through the trial balances, and sneak back out. Now, is everyone clear on the plan?" Alyson asked.

"I'm clear, but not really all that happy. There must be some way to get the information we need without going over to the dark side completely," Mac complained. "I've never even told a little white lie in my whole life. Well, not a serious one. I don't know if I can keep pulling off these whoppers."

"You'll be fine." Alyson hugged her. "Just remember, we're doing this so Santa can keep a little girl's Christmas wish."

As planned, they headed back to town hall right after the bookkeeper left for lunch.

"The hours of operation are from five p.m. until ten p.m. during the week and noon until eleven o'clock on Friday and Saturday night," the town hall receptionist was saying on the phone when Mac walked in. "Yes, sir, we did have an accident on the Ferris wheel earlier in the week, but I assure you every precaution is being taken to make sure that doesn't happen again."

Mac walked around the counter so the receptionist had to turn her back to the door in order to face her.

"We have twenty-four-hour security and all the rides are inspected daily," the receptionist continued.

"Excuse me." Mac raised her hand to get the receptionist's attention.

She looked at Mac but held up her forefinger, letting her know to wait. "No, sir, I don't know if the town will be sued over the accident. I certainly hope not. It's my understanding that no one was hurt."

Alyson slipped in while the receptionist was distracted by the phone call, which was from Trevor, and Mac's demand for attention at the counter. She silently moved through the reception area and into the bookkeeper's office, closing the door behind her.

"I see you're busy. I'll come back later," Mac called out, quickly leaving the office as soon as she saw Alyson was safely inside.

"Yes, it *would* further hurt the town's financial situation if we were to be sued." The receptionist continued to talk to Trevor as Mac walked out. "No, I don't know if I'll lose my job if cuts have to be made."

Alyson looked around the office. The blinds were closed, leaving the room dark, but she didn't dare turn on a light. Heading over to the file cabinet, she looked through each drawer until she saw a file labeled *Financial Statements* with folders for each month. Starting with November, she began looking for the dollar amounts that matched the circled withdrawals on the bank statements.

The amount circled on the November statement had been five thousand dollars. The trial balance was almost a hundred pages of individual entries, but only two of the entries were for that amount exactly. There was a five-thousand-dollar debit to community development, with a corresponding credit to cash, simply labeled *cash transfer*. There was another five-thousand-dollar expense under equipment lease, with a corresponding cash entry for a check to Cumberland Equipment.

In October, the only cash withdrawal was for thirty-five hundred dollars. There was a thirty-five-hundred-dollar entry under community development and another five-thousand-dollar entry under equipment lease, with a corresponding cash entry to Cumberland Equipment.

Okay, so there appears to be a five-thousand-dollar-a-month lease payment for some equipment, but the miscellaneous withdrawal is coded to community development. I wonder what they're using the money for and to whom the money is actually going.

Alyson checked another few months to see if the pattern continued. In September the cash amount changed to three thousand dollars. In August and then again in July there were corresponding cash withdrawals for three thousand dollars each to cash and community development. In June the pattern changed. There was no debit to community development and the cash withdrawal was for two thousand dollars. There were several debits for two thousand dollars, including one for maintenance. After comparing the statements for May and April, Alyson determined that the maintenance account was the one that corresponded with the cash withdrawal. The dollar amounts varied, but it appeared the withdrawals had started in the previous December.

She quickly went through each file to find the corresponding bookkeeping entry. The invoices that corresponded with the maintenance account originated from Tony's Lawn and Maintenance. There were no corresponding invoices for the entries made to community development. Alyson made a copy of a few of the invoices attached to the maintenance account, then rang Trevor's cell phone, which was his cue to once again distract the receptionist.

When Alyson peeked out of the office door, she could see the receptionist standing at the far side of the counter, flirting with Trevor. He had his boyish charm turned up to maximum magnetism, so Alyson was able to slip out undetected.

"So," Mac asked as soon as they reassembled in the parking lot, "did you find out where the missing money's been going?"

"Sort of. I'm not sure. I found the trial balance entries we were looking for, but I'm not sure I have any more of a solution to the mystery than I did before I started. I made copies of a few things. I thought we could go get some lunch and look through everything. We should have had you go in; you know what we're looking for better than I do," Alyson said to Mac.

"Me? No way. I'm firmly established in my role of distracto girl. You're much better at the whole espionage thing than I'll ever be."

"Yeah, maybe. But I'll need your help putting this all together. And Trevor, did you have to go so heavy on the charm? That poor woman will be blushing for a week."

"Hey, you said distract her, so I distracted her. Now let's get that lunch you suggested."

They headed over to Pirates Pizza and ordered their usual combo pizza and salad. The place was empty except for a couple with a small child in one of the booths near the door. They headed for the large booth in the back corner where they usually sat. Trevor got everyone's soft drinks while Alyson organized her notes.

"Basically," Alyson began when Trevor joined the girls, "I found a series of entries beginning in December of last year. The circled amounts varied between December and June, but all the entries were in the form of checks made out to Tony's Lawn and Maintenance."

"Those could have been legit expenses," Mac pointed out. "I'm sure the town has a need for a handyman to help with odd jobs. Did you find corresponding invoices?"

"Yes, and I made copies of a few of them. Most of the invoices were for things like painting, building repair, and yard maintenance."

"So why are we suspecting crooked dealings?" Mac reiterated.

"I'm not really saying the expenditures weren't on the up and up. The only reason I copied these invoices was because the checks were circled in red on the bank statements. I'm guessing someone had a reason to point them out."

"So what happened after June?" Trevor asked. "We had bank statements going all the way through November."

"In July the checks to Tony's Lawn and Maintenance stopped, but there was a new entry, a direct transfer of funds rather than a check, to a trial balance account labeled *community development*. I couldn't find any corresponding invoices or any indication of exactly to whom the funds went or what they were used for. The amounts also increased. In July through October each withdrawal was for three thousand dollars. In November it went up to five thousand dollars."

"The first step is to find out if Tony's Lawn and Maintenance is a legitimate company," Mac said.

"How do we do that?" Trevor asked.

"We start with the yellow pages. Go ask Mario if we can borrow his."

While Trevor went up to the counter to talk to the owner Mac looked more closely at the invoices. Most of them looked legitimate, although the dollar amounts seemed a little high for some of the services provided. One was for painting the town council chambers. Mac tried to remember whether the chambers really looked as if they'd had a new coat of paint. She'd have to check.

"Mario said our pizza would be ready in a few minutes." Trevor placed the borrowed phone book on the table. "He'll bring it over."

Mac looked in the yellow pages under lawn and maintenance and checked for Tony's in the business section of the white pages. "The company doesn't seem to be listed. Of course if it's a small business it may not have a separate line."

"It should have a business license, though," Alyson said. "Can you check for that, Mac?"

"Sure; I'll get my laptop out of the car."

While Mac was gone Mario delivered a piping hot, fully loaded pizza with layers of gooey cheese. Trevor put a slice on a plate for Mac, then helped himself to two.

"This really is the best pizza." Alyson took a bite of her own slice. "I'm not sure what they do to the sauce, but it's by far superior to most."

"I think the real secret is that everything is fresh. They make the sauce fresh every day and grate fresh cheese and slice fresh meat and vegetables. Nothing is ever frozen or packaged. And the crust—the crust is good enough to be its own food group."

"Okay, I'm back." Mac set her laptop on the table and looked around for an outlet to plug it in. After taking a few appreciative bites of her own slice of pizza, she opened the cover and started typing in commands. "Hey, that's weird."

"What's weird?" Alyson asked, wiping cheese from her chin.

"There's no business license issued to a Tony's Lawn and Maintenance. Why would the town hire an independent contractor that wasn't licensed?"

"Good question. Maybe that's why the checks were circled on the bank statements. Someone might have asked the same question. Who does the hiring anyway?" Alyson asked.

"I suppose the mayor, or possibly his secretary."

"Our two missing citizens," Trevor said.

"Can you do a general search on the Web for Tony's Lawn and Maintenance?" Alyson asked. "Maybe if he has a Web page or if he's run an ad in the paper at some point it will show up."

"Sure, no problem." Mac typed for several minutes. "I'm not getting anything. What about the invoices? Is there any information on them that might help us? A phone number? Address? Tax ID number?"

Alyson picked up one of the invoices. "No, nothing. Just the name of the business, the job performed, and the amount due. It looks like a homemade invoice, the kind you can make with any word processing program."

"The bookkeeper must have the information on file," Mac realized. "I mean, she had to send the check somewhere, and you're not supposed to issue a check without a tax ID number on file."

"Sounds like we need to pay another visit to the bookkeeper," Trevor suggested.

"It's too risky. Someone's going to suspect something if we hang around too much. Maybe we can trace the check through the bank. We have the check number and the bank account it was drawn on. Let me work on it before we resort to breaking and entering again. Besides, we still need to figure out where the withdrawals coded to community development actually went."

"Can you do that?" Alyson asked. "Hack into the bank's security system?"

"I can try. I managed to track the withdrawals from Barkley Cutter's account back to Jason Mastin last September. This shouldn't be any more difficult. At least give me until tomorrow to try."

"Okay. I guess we'd better get the candy we took the petty cash to pay for," Alyson said.

They picked it up and headed back to the town offices to turn the receipt and change in to the bookkeeper. It was almost three o'clock and the carnival crew was beginning to show up to prepare for the night ahead.

"Isn't that the guy from the Ferris wheel?" Trevor asked as they passed the section that contained the rides.

"Yeah. Hey, look, he's waving us over." Alyson waved back to him. "Let's see what he wants."

"I'm glad I ran into you," the man said when they walked up. "I saw the guy you were asking about again. The one who was arguing with the guy who must have been the mayor. I went to grab a bite and saw him having lunch with the bookkeeper I picked up a check from yesterday. It seemed a little odd, so I thought I'd mention it."

"That is odd," Alyson agreed. "Thanks for mentioning it. If you see him around again let us know."

"Sure thing. My daughter is insisting on going through the Santa house again tonight. I checked the schedule and saw you were working the first shift. Will the reindeer be there again? She was disappointed she didn't get a picture with him the first time."

"Sure, I'll bring him along," Alyson promised. "We'll see you tonight."

"So the bookkeeper skipped her spinning class today," Trevor said after the ride operator walked away.

"It doesn't really matter what she did during her lunch break," Mac responded. "The question we need answered is who that guy is, why he was arguing with the mayor, and how the bookkeeper is connected to him."

"I don't suppose we could just ask her?" Trevor suggested.

"If we start asking her a bunch of questions we'll just tip her off that we're snooping around," Alyson pointed out. "And we still might need to get into her office again, so we don't want her being extrasuspicious. I imagine the police are asking questions about the Ferris wheel accident and the disappearances as it is. My mom told me that she heard neither the mayor nor Mrs. Conway showed up for work today, pretty much ending speculation that they ran off for a weekend together. I'm sure the police are questioning everyone even remotely involved with either of them. I say we just keep our eye on her for now to see if we can find out who this mystery man actually is. We have a name from the mayor's messages. Let's start there."

They turned in the receipt and change, then headed home to change for their shift in the Santa house. Alyson put a change of clothes in her backpack for the play rehearsal immediately following their shift. After taking Tucker out for a brief run, she tied the reindeer antlers to his head and loaded him into her Jeep. Further investigation into what was turning out to be quite a complicated mystery would have to wait until the next day.

Chapter 11

In the morning they met for coffee and bagels at the Espresso Café, where they'd decided to gather to strategize their next moves. They had a lot of questions but few answers. Who was sabotaging the Christmas carnival? Who had tampered with the Ferris wheel, almost killing Alyson? What was the meaning of the circled checks and withdrawals on the bank statements found on the secretary's desk? Where were the mayor and his secretary? Why had the bookkeeper had lunch with the mayor's mystery visitor? Was Psycorp involved in everything that had been happening, and if so how? And why? Maybe the answers would somehow fit together in one big conspiracy; maybe they would prove to be isolated incidents.

"I've been thinking about the checks made out to Tony's Lawn and Maintenance." Alyson jumped right in once everyone was seated. "I think I have an idea of how to find out what account they were deposited into and, hopefully, who deposited them."

"How?" Mac asked before she bit into her seven-grain bagel.

"We call the bank to ask them. We'll need access to a town phone in case they have caller ID."

"You think they'll just give us the information over the phone?"

"They will if we ask them the right way. Here's my plan."

After they finished eating Alyson headed out to find Mr. Brownly. She had the file she'd taken from Mrs. Conway's desk tucked under her arm. Hopefully the bank statements contained all the information she would need to pull off her scam.

"Good morning, Mr. Brownly." Alyson greeted the middle-aged janitor with a huge smile. "I was wondering if you could let me in to the mayor's secretary's office to use the phone. There are more missing supplies for the carnival, and I volunteered to get on the phone to track them down." Alyson indicated the folder she held. "I have a whole list of calls to make and my cell phone is dead. I checked around, but most of the other phones are already being used. The mayor and his secretary aren't in today, so I thought I could make my calls there without inconveniencing anyone."

"Sure, no problem." Mr. Brownly started toward the administration building. "It's really strange, all the stuff that's been happening this week. I heard about the missing and damaged supplies, and then there was the whole fiasco with the toilets the other night. Seems to me we have a prankster in the house." He unlocked the door and let her in. "Come find me when you're done so I can lock up. It's real good of you to help out so much this week. I hope you can track down your supplies without too much trouble."

"Thanks. I shouldn't be long." Alyson headed over to the desk as he left, then searched through the drawers until she found a telephone book. Looking up the number for the bank, she placed her call from the secretary's phone.

"Hello. I'm calling from the bookkeeper's office at town hall. One of our vendors called to say he hadn't received his payment for work he did last summer. According to my records the check has cleared; I was hoping you could help me track down what account it was deposited into. Our vendor seems to think the check was deposited by someone other than himself."

"Do you have the account number of the check in question?" the bank clerk asked.

Alyson provided it.

"Okay, I've pulled up your account. Can you tell me the check number, who it was made out to, and the date it cleared?"

Alyson pulled out the June statement and gave the woman the check number. "It was made out to Tony's Lawn and Maintenance and it cleared on June 15."

"One moment, please."

Alyson waited as the clerk looked up the information. She glanced at the clock on the wall. She'd only been on the phone for two minutes; seemed longer.

"According to our records, the check was deposited into the account belonging to Tony's Lawn and Maintenance on the date indicated," the clerk informed her.

"Would it be possible to have a copy of the canceled check faxed over?" Alyson asked. "Our vendor is insisting he didn't receive the check. It would be nice to have proof that he did."

"Sure; what's your fax number?"

Alyson read off the number on the fax machine next to the desk.

"Okay, it should come through in a few minutes. Is there anything else I can help you with?"

"No; thank you for your help."

Alyson hung up and waited for the fax to come through. She decided to look around a little while she waited. On the desk was a photograph of the secretary's family; Mrs. Conway, an attractive man who must be her husband, and three children, including the little girl who'd come to the Santa house the other night. There were piles of paperwork, drawers of office supplies, and one with a small zippered bag with a brush and a lipstick. Alyson hesitated, then slipped the small brush into her pocket. Maybe if she and the mayor weren't found soon, she'd see if Chan, who owned an occult shop in town and had assisted them in solving another mystery, could help.

The phone on the fax rang and Alyson waited for the copy of the check to print, then slid it into her folder and went in search of Mr. Brownly. It was best not to take too long or arouse suspicion.

After she let the janitor know she was finished using the phone, Alyson hurried back to the parking lot, where the others were waiting for her.

"Well?" Mac asked.

"The check was deposited into an account belonging to Tony's Lawn and Maintenance. I got the bank to fax over a copy of the canceled check, but I haven't had a chance to look at it yet. Let's go somewhere else. We might look suspicious if someone sees us lurking around."

"My sisters are home today with a bunch of their friends or I'd suggest my house. We could go to the library," Mac suggested.

They headed there and settled around a table in a quiet corner of the foreign language section. Alyson pulled the copy of the canceled check from the folder and studied it for any type of clue. It was made out to Tony's Lawn and Maintenance, but there was no address. The memo on the bottom of the front of the check said *paint*. The back had the bank stamp and a hastily scribbled endorsement.

"I don't think this is going to tell us much." Alyson passed the check to Mac. "I was hoping there would be an address or something on it."

"Well, at least we have the account number. Maybe I can do something with that." Mac passed the check to Trevor.

"The signature isn't really legible, but doesn't this sort of look like an *A*?" Trevor pointed to a large squiggly mark.

"Yeah, I guess so," Mac agreed.

There was nothing but a wavy line following the squiggly mark. Another larger mark after it looked like a *G*, or maybe an *O*, followed by another wavy line.

"The name of the business is Tony's Lawn and Maintenance, so I'm betting the first letter is an *A* for Anthony," Trevor said. "Not that that helps us. There could be hundreds of Anthonys in town. It isn't an usual name."

Mac took the check from Trevor and looked it over again. "You know whose first name is Anthony and whose last name starts with a *G*? Mayor Gregor."

"Why would the mayor endorse the check? Unless he deposited the cash into his own dummy account." Trevor finally caught up with Mac's train of thought. "Of course. It's starting to make sense now. The mayor was embezzling money by submitting phony invoices from a dummy company.

Someone figured it out, thus the big red circles on the bank statement."

"Yeah, but why did things change in July?" Alyson asked. "The checks to Tony's Lawn and Maintenance stopped the same month the withdrawal to the community development account began. Why change his method of embezzling the money?"

"Maybe someone found out about it, so he mixed it up a little," Trevor suggested.

"If someone found out what was going on in June, why didn't that person report it?" Alyson asked.

"Maybe the mayor promised to repay the money if they kept quiet. If it was a friend of his, they might have gone along with the cover-up."

"Maybe." Alyson doubted Trevor's theory but didn't have a better one herself. "It still doesn't explain the other circled withdrawals. If they were legit why were they circled and why isn't there a better paper trail?"

Mac had sat quietly thinking during Alyson and Trevor's exchange. She studied the check again, looking at it from every angle, as if it somehow contained the answers they were looking for.

"It's not like we're bookkeepers or even have access to all the paperwork available. Maybe the community development thing is a separate item altogether."

"Yeah, but Trev ..." Alyson began when her cell phone rang.

"Hello? Sure, we'd be glad to. Really? That's okay; I have my credit card. Okay, see you then."

"Hey, guys," Alyson began, "I think we have a problem."

"What's wrong?" Trevor asked.

"That was my mom. She's downtown at the carnival and asked if we'd pick up some supplies for the snack bar. They're running a little low on some items. She asked if I had my credit card because we'd need to pay for the items and get reimbursed later. It seems the bookkeeper isn't there at the moment. And my mom said someone from the bank called to ask if the fax she sent came through all right. I bet they transferred the call to the bookkeeper."

"So she knows what we did. We're so totally busted. I knew this whole thing would end with my going to jail."

"It's okay, Mac," Alyson comforted her friend. "The bookkeeper has no way of knowing I was the one who requested the check. The bank clerk never asked for my name."

"So," Trevor surmised, "if the bookkeeper was that freaked out by the call she must know the significance of the check. She must be in on it with the mayor."

"Of course," Mac suddenly realized. "The bookkeeper found out what the mayor was doing. I mean, she's the bookkeeper; it makes sense she would notice any unusual expenditures. She confronted the mayor, but instead of turning him in, she decided she wanted in on the embezzlement. She knew checks leave a paper trail, so she changed the method of the embezzlement to a direct wire transfer and created the community development account. That also explains why the amounts increased. Each month's take had to cover two people. The question is, why was the mayor embezzling the money in the first place?"

"Didn't you tell me his wife took him for everything he had in their divorce?" Alyson contributed.

"Okay, this is all starting to make sense. Now for the million-dollar question: How does this fit in with the sabotage at the carnival and who's the no-good pond scum who defiled my Raquel?" Trevor asked.

"We've theorized before that Psycorp might be bribing someone to sabotage the carnival to make sure the land sale goes through," Mac reminded them. "Who better to bribe than the mayor? He owes the city an untold amount of money. The bookkeeper is blackmailing him. He must know on some level that he'll eventually get caught. Psycorp comes along and offers him a chunk of change if he pushes the sale through. He sees it as his opportunity to pay back the city and get out of a potentially messy situation."

"But Alyson could have been badly hurt when the Ferris wheel malfunctioned. If there'd been little kids in that bucket they might have been killed. Do you think the mayor could be that desperate?" Trevor asked.

"It's hard to say what someone who's been backed into a corner will do."

"Wait a minute," Alyson interrupted. "The Ferris wheel guy said the mayor was arguing with some guy the night the Ferris wheel was tampered with. Maybe the mayor didn't want to take that big of a step but his visitor pushed him into it."

"We need to find out who the man was and how he's connected to Psycorp," Trevor said.

"I have no way to know for sure that this is the same guy, but I still have the phone message with the name and phone number of someone who was supposed to be meeting with the mayor at the time of the argument. Let's give him a call," Alyson suggested.

She looked through the folder with the paperwork she had taken from the mayor's office. Then she took out her cell phone and dialed the number. "May I speak to Mr. Reinhart? I see. Do you know when he'll be in? Is there anyone else in his department I can speak to? Okay, thank you. No, that'll be all."

"So?" Mac asked.

"Carl Reinhart is the plant manager at Chemlab. He hasn't been in all week. The receptionist isn't sure when he'll be back in the office."

"You know, I remember there being a photo of the owner and plant manager of Chemlab when I found that article online about the investigation into the company. We could download it and ask the Ferris wheel operator if it's the same guy he saw arguing with the mayor."

"Good idea. Do you have your computer with you?"

"It's in the car. I'll go get it."

After downloading and printing the picture, they headed to the store to get the supplies Alyson's mom had requested.

"Thanks for doing this," Sarah said when they dropped off the items.

"Did the bookkeeper ever come back?" Alyson asked.

"No. And the way she just took off without speaking to anyone is really odd. The receptionist has been calling her cell phone, but she's not picking up. If she does show up I'll ask her about the procedure to get a reimbursement from a credit card. Are you kids in the Santa house again today?"

"Yes, first shift. Then we have play practice after that. It certainly has been a busy week."

"Well, I know everyone really appreciates your help, and I've heard so many nice things about the exceptional job you're doing in the Santa house. And it was such a good idea to bring Tucker. The kids love him."

"He loves all the attention, but I think he gets a little bored watching us rehearse for the play. Maybe we could cast him in a part. Did Scrooge have a dog?"

"I don't think so. If I get done before you tonight I'll pick him up and take him home with me," Sarah offered.

"Thanks. We've gotta run. See you tonight."

They stopped by the bookkeeper's office to confirm that she was still gone before going in search of the Ferris wheel operator.

"We really should ask him his name," Mac said as they looked around the carnival site. "We just keep referring to him as the Ferris wheel guy. Hey, isn't that him over there by the rocket ship to Mars?"

"Hey, guys, what's up?" the man asked as they approached.

"We wanted to ask if you'd look at a photo." Alyson handed him the printout. "Is one of these men the one you saw arguing with the mayor?"

"Yeah, the guy on the right. That's him all right. He was the one having lunch with the bookkeeper too. Odd that the mayor disappeared so soon after the argument. If you ask me, there's something fishy going on."

"Yeah, it seems like it. By the way, all the times we've talked, we never asked your name. I'm Alyson, and this is Mac and Trevor."

"People mostly just call me Tink."

"Like Tinkerbell?" Mac asked, surprised that such a large man would have such a tiny nickname.

"No, as in tinker. People say I'm always tinkering around with the equipment. I have a real feel for getting things adjusted just so. If one of the rides isn't operating just right they come find ol' Tink. I can make any piece of equipment purr like a kitten. That's why I'm so sure that someone intentionally caused the accident on the Ferris wheel. But don't you worry none. I've been checking every ride myself every day before we open."

"Well, thanks for your help, Tink." Alyson folded the paper and put it in her pocket. "Maybe we'll see you around tonight."

"So what now?" Mac asked as they walked away.

"How about lunch?" Trevor asked. "I'm starving."

"Trevor, it's way too early for lunch." Alyson looked at her watch. "Okay, maybe not, but seriously, it seems like all we do lately is eat. I'm up for getting something light. Not pizza. Maybe salad."

"There's a place nearby that has a great salad bar," Mac suggested. "It's close enough to walk."

"Sounds good. Lead the way."

Alyson's cell phone rang shortly after they started in the direction of the restaurant. "Wow, I seem to be popular today." She looked at the number. "Doesn't seem familiar, but it's local. Hello?" Alyson listened to the caller. "This is she. Yeah, I remember." Alyson raised her eyebrow in surprise. "Okay, when? Yeah, they're right here." She looked at her watch. "Okay, we'll be there."

"Who was it?" Mac asked.

"The detective from the cemetery last week. He said they have some new information and want to ask us a few more questions."

"Really. Like what?" Mac wondered.

"I have no idea. He asked if we could come by now. I guess lunch will have to wait. The police station is just down the street, though, so it shouldn't take too long."

They changed direction and walked toward the Cutter's Cove Police Station. The caller, Detective Redmont, was waiting for them near the front desk.

"We'll talk in the conference room," he said, and led the way. "Have a seat.

"We found out that the dead man in the cemetery wasn't a drifter but a college student from the University of Oregon. He was a chemistry major who was apparently on winter break. Now that the medical examiner has confirmed he was killed, we've stepped up our investigation and are reviewing previous statements and evidence. It seems you three have been in here quite a few times in the past few months."

"Are you accusing us of something?" Trevor asked.

"No, not accusing. It just seems that you have a tendency to be in the middle of things, and it occurred to me that you might know more about the dead student than I'd originally thought."

"We told you everything we knew," Alyson told him. "Trevor's car broke down, so we were walking through the cemetery to get to my house. We stumbled across the fresh grave and called you. Honestly, we didn't see anything else. Whoever killed the guy must have been long gone."

"It appeared the student had been camping in the area. Had you seen him there before?" the detective asked.

"I'd never even walked through the cemetery before. If the car hadn't broken down we wouldn't have been walking there that night."

The detective held up a picture and passed it around. "Have you ever seen this man before?"

"No," Alyson answered.

Mac and Trevor shook their head in agreement.

"Is this the victim?" Alyson asked.

"His name is Tim Driverton. He was a twenty-two-year-old grad student at the University of Oregon who was studying the effects of chemicals on the environment. He was last seen four days before you found his body. He told his roommate he was coming to the area to do research. The roommate was a little vague about exactly what it was he was researching, but he said it had something to do with proving something. Does any of this ring a bell? If you know something and aren't telling me, you could be putting yourselves in danger."

Mac made eye contact with Alyson. They both hesitated, unsure of how to proceed. Alyson shrugged and they both looked at Trevor, who was staring at them with a puzzled expression on his face.

Alyson started coughing. "I'm so sorry. Do you think I could get a glass of water? I've been fighting a cold lately."

"Sure, I'll be right back." The detective got up and went in search of a glass of water.

"What do we tell him?" Alyson whispered.

"Tell him about Chemlab but not the rest. Not yet, at least," Mac instructed.

"Huh?" Trevor asked.

"Shh. Here he comes." Alyson started coughing again.

"Here you are." The detective handed her a glass.

Alyson took a long drink. "Thank you; that's better."

"Now, about my original question…Can you think of anything at all you'd like to tell me? Any small piece of information could help."

"Well," Alyson hesitated, "when you mentioned the man was a chemistry student it made us think of the investigation that was done last year into the alleged mishandling of toxic waste by a Portland company, Chemlab. We found out that the owner of Chemlab is the same man who owns Psycorp, the company that's interested in buying the land where the body was found."

"Really? And how did you happen to find this out?"

"On the Internet," Mac told him. "We were interested in finding out more about Psycorp when they made the proposal to the town council to buy the land."

"Any theories about what the connection might be between Chemlab and the murdered student?"

"Maybe he had some kind of proof that would have reopened the investigation," Mac guessed.

"But how would an investigation into the illegal activities of a Portland-based company tie in with a piece of property in Cutter's Cove? I mean, if Chemlab would have been using the property as a dump site I think someone would have noticed. The cemetery is right off the highway," Redmont pointed out.

"I'm not sure," Mac defended herself. "I just found out that the murder victim was a chemistry grad student. I haven't had a chance to think it all out yet."

"Well, once you do, if you think you have anything, let me know."

He gave them all his business card again before they left the police station.

"The detective is doubtful, but I know there's a link between everything that's been going on and the dead chemistry student," Mac insisted. "I'm just not sure how it all fits together."

"I agree." Alyson walked between Mac and Trevor. "Let's get our lunch and put our brains together. I'm sure we'll figure it out."

The restaurant was packed with the midday lunch crowd, but they managed to find a table near the back. Alyson and Mac made huge salads from the all-you-can-eat soup and salad bar, while Trevor ordered a burger from the counter. The food was reasonably priced and served large portions, which made it popular with the high school kids. Trevor stopped to talk to several people from the football team as he made his way back to the table.

"This place is really hopping today," Mac commented as she waved at several people she knew. "Did you notice Shelly Longstrom's hair? She cut at least a foot off the length and bleached it bombshell blond. I didn't even recognize her at first."

Alyson turned around to look. "Wow, you're right; she looks totally different. It looks good, though. Different but good. Don't you think?"

"I guess. It'll take some getting used to. Shelly's had long dark hair for as long as I've known her. I wonder what Trevor will think. He dated her for a while when we were freshmen. I remember he used to talk about how much he liked her long hair. Where did he go anyway?"

"He's talking to Steve Rhodes and Sly Sullivan. I think I saw Chelsea walk in too. I'm sure when she spots him she'll come running."

"Actually, for the first time ever, I actually hope she does come over," Mac said. "She might have some news about the mayor. She was full of information the other day because her dad's a council member."

"It looks like you're getting your wish." Alyson nodded toward the front of the restaurant. "Here she comes with Trevor."

"Hey, guys, look who I ran into." Trevor sounded almost apologetic as he scooted into the booth, making room for Chelsea to sit next to him.

"How's it going, Chelsea?" Alyson asked.

"I can't stay long. I'm on my way to get my hair done, but I wanted to say hi. Jody and C. C. have pedicures scheduled this afternoon too, so we arranged to do lunch before our appointments. It's sad really; they're stuck in this oh-so-boring town for the whole break. I swear, if my parents weren't taking me to St. Croix next week I'd go totally insane before school starts back up on the fifth."

"Chelsea, how can you be bored?" Mac asked. "There's a ton of stuff going on with the carnival and other holiday events. Maybe if you got involved, maybe even volunteered, you'd enjoy it more."

"Are you kidding? That carnival is so lame. It was fun when I was five or six, but I grew up and learned to appreciate having some total hunk rub suntan lotion all over my body instead of sitting on some old guy's lap, asking for a bunch of toys that only break in a week anyway."

"Trevor is playing Santa this year," Alyson informed her.

"Really? Maybe I'll have to stop by for a little lap sitting after all. How about it, Trev? Want to make all my Christmas wishes come true?"

"I think I'll leave that to your lotion boy."

"What are you having done to your hair?" Alyson changed the subject.

"Just a trim and a blow dry. Hair should look natural, not overdone. Of course," Chelsea looked at Mac's long red braids, "a little styling never hurts. You know, Mac, you ought to think about adding a few layers to your hair. It would add body. And the braids," she shook her head, "scream elementary school."

"My hair is fine," Mac defended herself.

"Whatever. Did you see Shelly Longstrom's hair? I mean really. No one is going to buy the fact that she's a natural blonde. Besides the fact that pretty much everyone in town has known her most of her life, her coloring is all wrong for light hair. I mean, she didn't even bleach her eyebrows to match. She looks like a freak."

"I think she looks okay," Alyson said, "but I see what you mean about the eyebrows."

"Right?"

"By the way, have you heard any more about the mayor?" Alyson decided the chitchat portion of their conversation had gone on long enough.

Chelsea leaned in close and whispered, "I'm not supposed to say anything, but there was a major break-in at the mayor's house earlier today. I just found out about it before I came into town. Someone really trashed the place. His files were dumped all over his home office and his computer was totally missing. It's tragic really. My dad said the town just coughed up a bunch of money to pay for that fancy new computer."

"Do the police have any suspects?" Alyson asked.

"No, not yet. They think it might be related to the fact that Gregor's been totally AWOL since last Thursday night, and poor Mrs. Conway has completely disappeared. There's even some talk that Gregor came home and got his computer, then made it look like someone had broken in to cover his being there."

"Why would he do that?" Trevor wondered aloud.

"Who knows? I think there's more going on than anyone is saying. I wouldn't even know about the break-in at all if I hadn't been eavesdropping on a conversation my dad was having with one of the other council members."

"Did you hear anything else?" Mac whispered.

"I couldn't hear very well because the door to my dad's office was closed, but I got the feeling they've been suspicious about Gregor from even before he disappeared. My dad was saying something about the town deficit and why we're suddenly broke. I mean, if the town was in trouble, why wouldn't the mayor talk to the council about it before? And why was there a shortfall anyway? At the beginning of the year the budget was balanced and now the town's over thirty thousand dollars short? My dad was asking where the money went."

"Good questions. Is there a plan to do an audit?" Trevor asked.

"Yeah, after the first of the year. Everyone is busy with holiday plans at the moment." Chelsea looked at her watch. "Gosh, I gotta go. Ramon will have my head if I'm even one minute late." She got up from the booth and put her coat on. "I'll see you tonight, Trev. I'll be wearing a short skirt, so be sure your lap is nice and warmed up."

"Why did you have to tell her I was Santa?" Trevor groaned as she sauntered away.

"Sorry." Alyson laughed. "I didn't realize she'd make such a big deal about it."

"Are you kidding?" Mac joined in. "This is Chelsea. She makes a big deal about everything."

"So what do you make of the break-in at the mayor's place?" Alyson asked the others.

"I'm not sure, but I'm willing to bet it's related to everything else that's going on." Mac drummed her fingers on the tabletop as she thought. "It makes sense that the mayor would want to hide or destroy any evidence that might link him to the embezzlement. He must have found out that people were starting to ask questions about the missing money. Maybe Chelsea was right and he broke into his own house to hide the evidence while making it look like a robbery."

"Makes sense," Trevor agreed. "For all we know, the mayor might have flown the coop. He's looking at jail time if he's embezzling money and someone has enough evidence to prove it. I bet he'll be tanning in some South American country before you know it."

"It'd be the smart thing to do." Mac nodded. "Chelsea said that the deficit is over thirty thousand dollars. By our calculations, that's just about the amount the mayor has embezzled in the past year. And the bookkeeper's not in the clear either, if we're right and she's involved."

"This whole thing is getting more and more complicated by the hour." Alyson rubbed her forehead. "It's giving me a headache."

"We came here to brainstorm." Mac pulled a pad out of her purse. "Let's get started. The sooner we solve this mystery the sooner we can get on with presents and eggnog. I haven't even done my Christmas shopping yet."

"Okay, where do we start?" Trevor rubbed his hands together, anxious to get down to work.

"Let's make three separate lists," Mac suggested. "One list will be things we know, another things we suspect, and the last one things we don't know but want to find out. We'll start with what we know."

"We know a chemistry student was found murdered at the old cemetery and that Psycorp wants to buy the land the cemetery sits on," Alyson started.

"We also know Psycorp and Chemlab are owned by the same person and that Chemlab was investigated for toxic waste violations last year," Mac added.

"We know someone—a dirty, rotten someone— violated poor Raquel," Trevor joined in. "We also know someone is sabotaging the carnival and almost killed us all when they tampered with the Ferris wheel. And finally, we know the mayor and his secretary are missing and Santa promised a little girl he'd try to bring her mommy home."

Mac stopped writing and placed her hand over Trevor's. "Don't worry, we'll find her. Or at least we'll try. I think we all want to see that little girl's Christmas wish granted." She returned to her pad. "Anything else we know?"

"If you can believe Chelsea, we know someone broke into the mayor's home office and the town council is beginning to get suspicious about the missing money," Alyson contributed.

"Yeah, we know the mayor was embezzling money, creating this whole mess in the first place," Trevor accused.

"Actually," Mac corrected, "we *suspect* the mayor was embezzling money. We found the bank statements, and the endorsement on the checks made out to what we suspect is a phony company looks like it might be the mayor's, but we don't actually have any proof yet."

Mac wrote a note about the mayor possibly embezzling money on the second page under things they suspected.

"Is there anything else we know before we move on to things we suspect?" Mac asked.

"We know the mayor was arguing with the plant manager from Chemlab the day of the Ferris wheel accident, and we suspect he had something to do with the accident," Alyson added.

"Okay, anything else?"

"We suspect the bookkeeper found out about the mayor embezzling money and is blackmailing him in order to get her own piece of the pie." Alyson thought a minute. "We also suspect someone from Psycorp is either blackmailing or bribing someone to sabotage the carnival. Probably the mayor."

"Anything else we suspect?" No one added anything, so Mac turned to the third page to add things they wanted to find out.

"We don't know why Psycorp would want that particular piece of land bad enough to sabotage the carnival," Alyson pointed out. "I think that's the main thing we're missing in our theory that they're involved: motive."

"Okay, let's talk about that," Mac said. "Say I'm the owner of Chemlab, a large, well-established chemical plant that already has most of the farmers in the area as customers. I want to buy a piece of property less than an hour or so from my current plant, but I know the bad publicity over last year's investigation might hamper the sale of the property. I create a new company, and to throw everyone off, I create a series of diversions concerning its origin. The question is why? Why would I want the property in the first place, and why would I lie to get it? Most important, why would I risk the reputation of the business I already own to sabotage a local carnival?"

"People are usually the most motivated to do anything by greed or fear," Alyson pointed out.

"Okay, say I think this particular piece of property will bring me great wealth, more than any other property in the area," Mac speculated.

"Does anyone remember my buried treasure theory?" Trevor asked. "Or maybe that particular piece of property has a tunnel entrance that leads directly into the vault at the Cutter's Cove Community Bank. It's not impossible, you know; we've found other tunnels in the area. Better yet, maybe the cemetery is sitting directly on top of the largest vein of gold on the West Coast."

"Although I greatly value your input, Trev, I don't think any of those ideas will really prove to be the motive. The correct solution is usually the simplest one. A buried treasure is really a long shot," Alyson said.

"Okay, do you have a better idea?"

"Fear. The only reason I could see for the owner of Chemlab to risk everything is the fear of something happening or being discovered. The dead student was a chemistry major. Chemlab was investigated for toxic waste violations, which would have put the owner in prison if it could have been proven. I think the chemistry student was on to something, and it probably involved the land where he died."

"Like maybe they've been burying toxic waste in the cemetery?" Mac guessed.

"Maybe, although that seems unlikely. The detective was correct when he pointed out that someone would have noticed large trucks pulling up with loads of toxic waste and burying them in the cemetery. Besides, there haven't been new graves there for over a hundred years, so someone would for sure notice freshly dug-up dirt, just like we did."

"So what then?" Trevor asked.

"I'm not sure. Mac, you're almost as much of a genius in the chemistry lab as you are on the computer. Maybe we can get some soil samples and you can test them for any nasties that might be present."

"Sure, I could do that. It's getting late today and we're due at the Santa house in under an hour. We could get the samples tomorrow morning."

"Okay, that's a plan. If the soil is tainted we just need to figure out how to tie it to Chemlab and, ultimately, everything else that's been going on. I think I feel that headache coming on again."

They hurried home to change their clothes and get Tucker the reindeer. With only minutes to spare, they ran across the parking lot and let themselves into the Santa house.

"Someone forgot to turn on the heater." Mac shivered. "It's freezing in here."

"It's not so bad," Trevor said.

"Not for you; you have on twenty pounds of clothes, but Aly and I are practically naked. I think this elf is going to have to wear her coat until it warms up."

"Elves don't wear coats," Trevor argued.

"This one does."

"This one too," Alyson agreed. "Hey, here comes my mom."

"Hi, guys," Sarah greeted them as she hurried in. "I just wanted to let you know I wasn't able to get your reimbursement today because the bookkeeper never came back to her office. Everyone is really starting to worry. Not only is she missing but her office was broken into and her computer and a lot of her files are missing. The police have been there all afternoon. First the mayor, then his secretary, and now the bookkeeper. What in the world is going on?"

"Uh, Mom…there's something we have to tell you."

"I figured as much."

After Alyson, Mac, and Trevor finished both their shift in the Santa house and play rehearsal, they headed over to Alyson's to fill her mom in on everything that had been happening. Alyson realized she should have brought her mom into the loop before this. She had helped them to solve other mysteries and was great about keeping her calm and not freaking out, the way most moms usually did.

Sarah had waited around until after their shift was over so she could take Tucker home with her while the kids had rehearsal. Alyson had mentioned that they'd never had time for dinner, so her mom even promised to have something waiting for them to eat when they got home.

"My mouth is watering at the thought of one of your mom's home-cooked meals." Trevor licked his lips. "Heck, after the crazy pace of the past few weeks, I'd be excited about getting one of *my* mom's home-cooked meals, and those mostly come from a can."

"I know what you mean." Alyson yawned as she drove toward her oceanfront home. "My mom hasn't cooked since the carnival began."

"At least your mom cooks," Trevor insisted. "My mom's specialty is reheating."

Once they were gathered around the kitchen table and the food had been served, Alyson filled her mom in on the events of the past couple of weeks. Mac had brought the notes they'd made that afternoon, detailing what they knew, what they suspected, and what they needed to find out.

"We're planning to go out to the cemetery to get some soil samples tomorrow," Alyson informed her mom. "If we can prove there's contamination present, maybe the police will believe our suspicion that Chemlab is somehow involved in this whole thing."

"If whoever is behind this kidnapped the mayor, his secretary, and the bookkeeper and is responsible for the accident on the Ferris wheel and the murdered student, they're obviously pretty dangerous," Sarah pointed out. "You kids need to be extracareful. Be sure to take Tucker with you tomorrow, and keep your cell phones charged and accessible."

"We'll be careful," Alyson promised. "This whole thing is really bizarre. I mean, who would have thought the mayor would be embezzling money or that the bookkeeper was probably in on it?"

Mac sighed. "Ten days ago my biggest concern was what to get Eli for Christmas, and now I'm wondering what happened to poor Mrs. Conway and whether the mayor will go to prison and where our investigation into Chemlab's activities will lead. Suddenly I'm wishing this was all a dream and I'll wake up tomorrow to a day of cookie baking and watching *A Charlie Brown Christmas*, not trying to prove a motive for murder."

Alyson put her arm around Mac's shoulders. "I'm not sure I can help with the baking part, but we taped *A Charlie Brown Christmas* the other night. Let's watch it now and pretend for a little while that everything isn't about to come apart in a big way."

"I'm in." Trevor stood up from the table. "I'll even do the Snoopy dance. I do it every year for Mac. It's like our own personal best-friend tradition."

Chapter 12

The next morning Mac and Trevor met at Alyson's house on the way to the cemetery. Alyson had made a fresh pot of coffee to go with the blueberry muffins her mom had whipped up sometime earlier.

"Oh, muffins." Trevor grabbed one and bit half of it off. "With yummy crumblies on the top," he mumbled as he chewed.

"I think I'll just stick with coffee." Mac sat down at the table and poured a generous helping of milk in her cup. "My stomach feels a little rumbly this morning."

"I hope you're not getting sick." Alyson felt her friend's forehead in a motherly way.

"No, it's just nerves. I think this is all getting to me a little, but not to worry; I'm fully committed to finding the bad guys and locking them away for a good long time. I guess I'm mostly worried about Mrs. Conway. My gut tells me she's an innocent bystander in all this. I feel like we should be doing more to find her. I mean, I know the police are working on it, but quite frankly, my faith in them is more than a little shaky."

"I know what you mean. I'm not sure what we can do to help, though. Oh, wait, I have an idea." Alyson got up from the table and ran up the stairs to her room. She came down several minutes later carrying a small blue travel brush. "I sort of borrowed this from Mrs. Conway's desk while I was using the phone. I forgot all about it until now."

"How's a brush going to help us?" Trevor asked.

"Chan," Mac answered enthusiastically. "I lay awake all night trying to figure out something I could do to help find her. You're a genius. Let's go see him right after we finish at the cemetery."

"We could go first if you want."

"No, the cemetery is between here and town. We might as well get the samples on the way; then we can go to my house to test them after we talk to Chan."

"I hope he's a bit more direct this time." Trevor took his third muffin from the plate.

"He told us it's different every time. Maybe this time things will be clearer," Alyson defended him.

"An address would be nice," Trevor added.

"Okay, let's go." Mac got up from the table.

"Hey, I'm still eating," Trevor protested.

"Take one with you. It's getting late and we have a lot to accomplish before our shift at the Santa house."

The cemetery looked a lot different during the day than it had at night. The ground was desolate, barren except for a few weeds and some dead trees. Most of the headstones were broken and faded, many lying on the ground after years of neglect. The winter sun shone brightly on the ocean surface beyond the cliffs. A cold wind whistled over the bluff, causing the air to feel much colder than it actually was.

"Do we have any visitors?" Mac asked.

"No, not today. It's just us. Where do we start?"

"We need to gather samples from a large area. Use these test tubes I brought," Mac instructed the others. "Fill each one, cap it, then label the approximate location where you took the sample. For example, I'll label this one Max Kegan's grave. We should divide the area into about twenty sections and take a sample from each one. Trevor, you start with the sections closest to the road, I'll do these in the middle, and Alyson can get the ones closest to the water."

Trevor stood looking at the test tubes Mac had handed him.

"Hop, hop," she commanded. "We haven't got all day."

"Yes, sir." Trevor saluted Mac, then marched away.

"Before you yell at me, I'm already gone." Alyson started walking toward the edge of the bluff, with Tucker following behind her.

It took almost two hours to gather and label all twenty samples. By the time they were finished Trevor was ready for lunch.

"After we stop by Chan's," Mac reminded him. "I've heard guys have a one-track mind; I just didn't know it was for food."

"Oh, it's not," Trevor kidded. "But I'm here in a cemetery with my two female *friends*, so food will have to do."

As it turned out, Chan's occult shop was closed when they went by, so they ended up eating first.

"Does that guy even have regular business hours?" Trevor asked. "He's been closed half the times we've gone there."

"I think he's pretty much open when he's open and closed when he's not. It is a little frustrating, though," Mac agreed. "Of course, if you complained about it he'd just say something like 'everything in its time. No sooner, no later.'"

"We'll check back after lunch," Alyson said. "I'm thinking deli."

"How about we get deli sandwiches and go back to my house? We can test the samples after we eat, then check back at Chan's."

"Sounds fine with me. How about your brother and sisters—should we bring them something?"

"No, they went shopping with my mom today. They won't be back until this evening. She wanted me to go, so I had to make up an excuse not to. I told her I was having trouble with my lines for the play and needed to practice before tonight."

They stopped at the deli for sandwiches, then headed over to Mac's. The chemistry supplies she kept on hand were up in her room, so she went up to get them while Alyson set out the food and Trevor wolfed down chips.

Mac carefully set everything up to test the samples before stopping to inhale her salami sandwich.

"You better slow down or you'll get indigestion," Alyson warned as she nibbled on her turkey sandwich, tossing a piece of the bread to Tucker, who waited patiently at her feet.

Mac put her sandwich down and walked over to the things she'd brought downstairs and started mixing chemicals. "I'll be fine. I'm just anxious to get started. Testing each of these samples for the various kinds of chemicals that might be present will take some time. In fact, we might not find anything at all. Not on the first try. Even if chemicals were dumped in the cemetery we'd have to pretty much test that exact spot. I mean, there's some shifting of the dirt by the wind, but ... oh, hey. Look at that."

"What?" Alyson set her sandwich down and joined Mac, who was looking through a microscope.

"This dirt is testing positive for everything. There's no way that happened naturally; someone dumped a bunch of really nasty chemical waste here."

"You're kidding. I mean, I know you're not kidding, but honestly, I was doubtful we'd find anything, and after your speech—well, I didn't think it would be that easy."

"Me neither. The thing is, the dirt looked like it hadn't been disturbed in forever. When could someone have dumped this stuff? And how? This sample was taken right off the highway."

"Maybe there was an accident on the highway and the spill occurred naturally. We'd better test the rest of the samples to see if the contamination is widespread."

It took a good part of the afternoon to test all the samples. Many of them were totally clean, or at least clean enough that natural contamination from an industrial society could explain it. Other samples were like the first, heavily contaminated, while still others showed signs of unnatural contamination but not to the degree of the first sample. Mac drew a rough sketch of the cemetery and plotted the various degrees of contamination. "It looks like the heaviest contamination runs along a sort of winding line. Like a truck drove around the cemetery in a squiggly pattern as it dumped the waste."

"That doesn't make any sense," Trevor said.

"No, it doesn't. We need more samples. Maybe if we test areas we haven't sampled yet a clearer pattern will emerge. Let's go by Chan's first. If he's not there we'll head back over to the cemetery. I'd better put this stuff away before my mom gets home," Mac added. "There's no way I could explain why I was using chemistry to learn my lines for the play."

Chan was dusting the shelves of magic books when they arrived. As usual, the counters were covered with jars of newt eyeballs, chicken feet, frog legs, and other various parts of long-deceased animals. Alyson enjoyed visiting the unusual shop.

"Alyson, so good to see you. Sorry about the mess. I'm doing a bit of spring cleaning."

"But it's December," Trevor reminded him.

"No use waiting until the last minute. Now, what can I do for you?"

"Have you heard about the missing town employees? The mayor, his secretary, and, most recently, the bookkeeper."

"No, I've been away for the past week. I just returned a few hours ago. You say the mayor and his staff are missing?"

"Yes," Alyson explained. "The mayor and his secretary have been missing since at least last Friday. We're especially concerned about the secretary. The mayor may be away of his own volition, but we're afraid the secretary has met with foul play. We were hoping you could get a reading off this brush. I took it from her desk."

"I can try. Why is it that you feel the mayor's disappearance isn't foul play but the secretary's is?"

Alyson gave him enough details to suggest the suspected embezzlement and stolen computer and files without revealing too much. "It looks like he might be trying to destroy evidence and disappear before he ends up in prison."

"Possibly, but things aren't always as they appear. I'd keep an open mind. Now for the secretary; let's see what you have."

Chan held the brush in his hands and closed his eyes. It appeared he had gone into a trancelike state. He was totally still, barely breathing. Alyson watched his face, which appeared emotionless.

"I see a middle-aged woman with short dark hair. She is injured, frightened. She is alone in a dark place. It is a small space, like a closet, or possibly a storm shelter."

Chan continued to concentrate while the others held their breath. "I am sensing that she is underground, yet near the surface. I would look for her in a small storm shelter or root cellar."

"Anything else?" Mac asked anxiously.

"There is a building nearby, or possibly the shadow of a building."

"The shadow of a building?" Alyson asked.

"I sense the building, but the feeling seems hollow, without depth or texture, like a shadow."

"What kind of building?" Trevor asked.

"A barn, perhaps. White. I'm not sensing life. I believe it's deserted."

"Okay, so where is this barn?" he pushed. "There are hundreds of barns in this area, lots of them white."

"I can hear the sound of the ocean. Waves crashing. There is something else I can't quite make out. Something near the barn, in front of the door. Something small. Something old; long ago abandoned."

Chan meditated for several more minutes before opening his eyes. "I'm sorry; that is all."

"Do you ever just come up with an address?" Trevor asked. "'Cause an address would be really helpful."

"I am sorry. That is not how these things work. I get flashes, images, sometimes nothing more than impressions. It is for the seeker to understand. Your emotions allow you to see what is yours to see."

"Thanks for your help." Alyson offered Chan a piece of paper. "If you think of anything else call me."

"I sensed that she was nearby. I would check out abandoned farms in the area," Chan added as they walked out.

They climbed into Alyson's Jeep and sat thinking for a moment.

"The Thompsons' farm is abandoned, but their barn is red," Mac offered.

"I'm not really familiar with the area," Alyson said. "Any other ideas?"

Mac and Trevor racked their brains for an answer.

"Chan mentioned the sound of the ocean, so it must be one of the farms along the coast highway. Why don't we take a drive to see what we find?" Trevor suggested. "I'll drive; I'm more familiar with the area than you are."

"Good idea. We'll just look for a deserted farm with a white barn." Alyson turned the heater on high. "It's getting late; we'd better hurry."

Most of the farms they passed along the highway were clearly occupied. They followed dirt roads that veered off toward the coast and didn't have obvious occupants until there were either signs of inhabitants or a barn that was other than white.

"It's going to be dark soon," Mac observed.

"Let's go a few more miles," Trevor said. "We're getting pretty far away from town and Chan said it wasn't far. Maybe his vision was a dud."

"Go back. Try that road." Alyson pointed to the left.

"What road?" Trevor slowed down and began to back up but couldn't see where Alyson wanted him to turn.

"The one over by that tree."

Trevor inched toward where Alyson was pointing. "I don't see a road, just a lot of sagebrush."

"I know it doesn't look like much, but I swear I saw a road when we passed by."

"Okay, let's check it out." Trevor put the Jeep into four-wheel drive and slowly drove over the hard-packed dirt and brush in the direction Alyson indicated.

"Stop here." Alyson jumped out.

"I don't see any buildings, Aly," Trevor pointed out.

"No, but there's a foundation." Alyson hurried over toward the edge of the bluff where the foundation of a building was clearly visible. "And an abandoned tricycle," she added.

"Why did Chan see a barn if there isn't one?" Trevor asked.

"He said he felt he saw the shadow of a barn. Maybe he saw the farm as it once was. Look around for a storm door. It's probably covered in brush, so look carefully," Alyson instructed.

The barren landscape was barely visible in the fading light. A cold wind whistled over the bluff, as if moaning in sorrow, as it coiled its way through the scattered remnants of previous residents long forgotten. A rusted tricycle, a stone foundation, the skeleton of a crumbling chimney, broken glass, bits and pieces of abandoned dreams.

"It's getting dark," Mac worried. "Do you happen to have a flashlight in your Jeep?"

"Check the glove box. I think there's one in there."

Alyson stopped to listen. She closed her eyes and opened her mind to any impressions waiting to be acknowledged. She felt herself being drawn toward a mound of dirt near what must be the remains of the original farmhouse. She carefully made her way across the parched earth, walking slowly so as not to miss the clue she was being led toward.

"I found it," Alyson yelled, "but it's locked. Mrs. Conway, are you in there? Can you hear me?" Silence greeted her inquiry. "We need to find something to break the lock."

"Yeah, but what?" Trevor looked around at the abandoned property.

"Wait; I've got it." Alyson ran toward her Jeep as Mac continued to call Mrs. Conway's name.

"God, I don't hear a thing. I hope she's not already dead."

Alyson drove the Jeep over to the spot where Mac was on her knees, calling Mrs. Conway's name. She took a rope out of the vehicle and tied one end to the latch on the door and the other to the vehicle's frame.

"Oh, I get it; you're going to pull the door open with the Jeep." Trevor took the rope from her. "Let me. I hope it's long enough. It won't work if we can't get enough power behind the lunge forward. Okay, punch it." Trevor stood back, holding Mac against his chest.

The Jeep lunged forward, the slack in the rope tightened, and the lock tore free. Mac ran over to the now gaping opening to the cellar and looked inside the small room.

"Mrs. Conway, are you in there?" Mac looked up. "I see her. She's not moving. I'm going in."

Mac slid carefully into the partially collapsed cellar and used her fingers to feel for a pulse. "She's alive, but barely. Call for help."

"I already did." Alyson came up behind her. "Do you think we should try to get her out of there?"

"I don't think we should move her until help arrives. She's hurt. I'm not sure how bad, but I'd hate to hurt her further."

"It shouldn't be long. I'll take the Jeep and go out to the road so the ambulance doesn't miss the nonexistent road," Trevor offered.

It was less than ten minutes before Alyson heard the sound of distant sirens. "I'd better call my mom to see if she can get another team to work the Santa house. There's no way we'll get there in time."

It was after six o'clock by the time the emergency crew had taken Mrs. Conway to the hospital and the police had interviewed them about how they'd come to find her. Alyson made up a story about taking a wrong turn, getting lost, and hearing someone call for help. She doubted Chan would mind if she told the police how they'd really found her, but she was afraid the true story would raise more questions than she was willing to answer.

"We only have an hour until rehearsal," Alyson said as they drove back into town. "Maybe we should get a quick bite to eat. I'm starving. The café downtown is usually pretty quick."

"Sounds good." Mac nodded. "It's been quite a day. I'm exhausted. But relieved. I'll probably sleep better tonight, knowing Mrs. Conway is safe in the hospital."

"How did you know where to turn?" Trevor asked Alyson.

"The first time we drove by I swear I saw a road. It was clear as day. But when we went back it was gone. Honestly, I have no explanation. I'm probably losing my mind."

"Chan did say our emotions would show us the way," Mac reminded them. "And you're always seeing ghosts; why not the ghost of a road? Is it weird? Seeing things the rest of us don't see?"

"Yeah, sometimes. I certainly never asked to see ghosts or have prophetic dreams, but I've accepted it. I've helped a lot of people, and although it's sometimes scary, I wouldn't change a thing."

"Yeah, I guess you're right. I do feel good about helping poor Mrs. Conway. Who do you think did that to her?"

"Maybe she'll tell us when she wakes up. We'll check with the hospital tomorrow to see if she can have visitors." Alyson pulled into the parking lot of the festively decorated café. "We'll be back in a jiffy, Tucker, and I'll bring you a treat."

The dog curled up in the cargo area to wait.

"Wow, they really went all out with the Christmas cheer," Trevor commented. "Someone must have spent an entire day hanging all those lights."

"I could use some holiday cheer," Alyson responded as they were shown to a table by the window. "With all of the stuff that's been going on I haven't had a chance to really relax and enjoy the season at all. I love what they've done with the tables. The centerpieces with the evergreen branches and red carnations look really nice on the white tablecloths."

"Yeah, it's nice." Mac glanced at her menu as "Winter Wonderland" played in the background. "I'd better have some coffee or I'll never make it through rehearsal. In fact, I think I'll do the whole breakfast thing and order an omelet to eat. They serve breakfast all day here."

"Breakfast sounds good." Alyson nodded. "And I wouldn't turn down a little caffeine myself. How about you, Trev? Are you going to do the breakfast thing too?"

"Sure, why not? They have a meat lover's omelet with sausage, bacon, and ground beef. Throw in four eggs and you have a cholesterol feast made in heaven."

Chapter 13

First thing next morning they headed over to the hospital in the hope of visiting with Mrs. Conway. A phone call earlier had revealed that she was conscious, comfortable, and doing quite well now that she'd been given fluids. Her injuries were actually minor compared to her severe dehydration. It was expected that she'd be able to go home by the weekend.

"Mrs. Conway." Alyson stuck her head around the open door. "I'm here with Trevor and Mackenzie. We were hoping to visit you for a few minutes if you're feeling up to it."

"Please come in. I don't know how I can ever thank you kids for finding me. The doctors say I probably wouldn't have lasted much longer. I'm not sure how you managed to find me when the police couldn't, but I'll be forever grateful."

Alyson sat down on the chair next to the bed while the others hung back. "We're glad we could help. We were wondering if you were up to telling us what happened. We've been looking into a few other things that have happened in the past couple of weeks and we think your kidnapping could be related."

"Of course." Mrs. Conway smiled weakly. "Anything I can do." She adjusted her position in the bed so she was sitting up straighter. "I was driving home on Friday night after work. A black truck ran me off the road. When I came to a stop, a man jumped out of the truck and yanked open my car door. He hit me in the face and I blacked out. I woke up in the storm cellar. I'm afraid that's all I really remember. I screamed at the top of my lungs in the beginning, but no one heard me. I really thought I was going to die in that cellar. I have no idea how long I was trapped in there, but it seemed like an eternity. I'm not sure I ever want to be in the dark again. My husband has already gone out to buy night-lights for all the rooms in the house, including our bedroom."

"Did you recognize the man in the truck?" Alyson asked.

She shook her head. "He had on one of those full-face ski masks. He was kind of tall, though. Over six feet."

"Do you have any idea who might have wanted to hurt you?"

"I don't have any enemies that I know of. I've been told the mayor is missing too. I do hope someone can find the poor man soon. Being alone in a small, dark space is no way to die."

"There was a folder on your desk with copies of bank statements in it. We found it when we were searching for clues as to your whereabouts. Can you tell us what you know about that?"

"Dr. Went, one of the town council members, gave me the folder on Friday morning. He'd come to speak to Mr. Gregor about the contents of the folder, but when I told him the mayor wasn't in he left it with me. I have no idea why he'd requested copies of the statements from the bank or why some of the withdrawals were circled, but when I asked Marge Cranston, the bookkeeper, about it she seemed sort of bothered. She said she didn't know anything about the circled entries, but she had a shocked look on her face. I had the impression she knew more than she was letting on. Do you think those papers are connected to my abduction?"

"We're not sure. Maybe. We need to look into a few things, but we'll let you know what we find out. If they are connected Dr. Went may be in danger. Do you know how to get a hold of him?"

"He was on his way out of town for the holiday when he dropped the folder off. He didn't tell me where he was going, but he did say he wouldn't be back until after the first of the year."

"We'll let you get some rest now. We're so glad you're okay. If we don't see you again before, have a wonderful holiday with your family."

"Oh, I will. The best." She paused for a moment, then added, "I'm not one to look a gift horse in the mouth, but why were you looking for me? Not that I'm not enormously grateful, but you don't even know me."

"Trevor is playing Santa this year. Your daughter made a Christmas wish for Santa to bring her mommy home. We had to try; Santa likes to keep his promises."

"Well, I'll be. I'm going to have to give that angel an extra hug when I get out of here. Thank you again for everything."

"So what now?" Trevor asked as they exited the hospital into the crisp December air.

"We still need to go back to the cemetery to get another batch of dirt samples," Mac reminded him. "I can stop by my house to pick up some test tubes and the list of areas we wanted to get samples from. My brother and sisters are home today, though, so maybe I should get my stuff and we can go back to Alyson's to run the actual tests. It'll be a lot less chaotic there."

"Sounds like a plan," Alyson said. "We'd better hurry; it looks like it might rain."

They picked up everything Mac needed at her house and headed over to the cemetery for the second time in as many days. The sky had darkened considerably since they'd first emerged from the hospital. Mac gave the others test tubes and their site assignments and everyone got to work gathering samples. A loud clap of thunder echoed off the cliff walls as a storm approached. Alyson looked westward across the ocean toward the storm in the distance. Something caught her eye and she walked to the edge of the bluff and looked down. The tide was out farther than Alyson had ever seen it. Huge rocks that were usually covered by the rough surf were completely exposed.

"Hey, guys," Alyson called the others over. "Check it out. The tide's really low today."

Mac and Trevor came over and peered over the edge of the bluff with her.

"Where's that water coming from?" Trevor asked. "The tides way out, yet there's a steady flow of water from the ground. It looks like a river that just magically appeared from the side of the cliff."

"I think it *is* a river," Mac confirmed. "An underground river. It's usually covered by twenty feet of water, so you'd never notice it. If the water's contaminated it would totally explain our weird contamination pattern. We need to get a sample before the tide comes back in."

"Yeah, but how do we get down there?" Alyson asked. "The first step off the side of this cliff would be quite a doozy."

"I think I can get down there," Trevor said. "Do you still have that rope? We'll tie one end around the frame of the Jeep and I'll tie the other around my waist in case I slip."

"I have the rope, but are you sure you want to do this? It's a pretty sheer drop and the rocks won't be forgiving if you fall."

"It'll be a piece of cake. We better hurry, though; the storm is getting closer."

Trevor tied the rope around his waist while Alyson tied the other end to the frame of the Jeep. Mac labeled several test tubes and put them in Trevor's sweatshirt pocket.

"Remember," she instructed, "try to get clean samples. Water only, no soil."

"Will do." Trevor took a minute to pick out the best route to take for his climb down, then slid over the edge of the cliff.

Trevor's journey to the bottom was a slow one. Each step he took needed to be carefully placed. Alyson and Mac watched as showers of small rocks fell to the ground below as his footsteps disturbed the fragile cliff face. Every few minutes thunder from the approaching storm shook the ground below their feet. After what seemed like an eternity, they saw him reach the bottom and set to work gathering the samples.

"That lightning is really getting close." Mac bit her lip nervously. "If it hits the water the charge will carry through it for quite a distance. I hope Trevor's clear of it by now. I'm too nervous to look."

Alyson looked over the edge. "He's about a third of the way up. He'd better hurry; the tide's coming back in. You can't even see the rocks he was just standing on anymore."

Mac looked out toward the quickly approaching storm. "He's taking too long. The storm is going to get here before he climbs all the way up. Oh, God. He just slipped. His feet are in the water."

"Trevor," Alyson yelled as loud as she could, "you have to get out of the water."

"I'm trying, but the rocks are more slippery than I thought they'd be. I can't get a foothold."

A bolt of lightning flashed horizontally across the sky.

"Trevor!" Mac's scream was drowned out by a deafening explosion of thunder.

"It's okay. The lightning didn't hit the water." Alyson hugged her friend. "We have to get him out of there. Trevor," Alyson called, "I'm going to pull you up. Hang on to the rope and try to walk your way up the wall as I pull."

"Okay," Trevor called back.

"Keep an eye on him," Alyson instructed Mac. "Yell real loud if he gets in trouble. I'm going to pull him up with the Jeep."

Alyson ran to the Jeep and, making sure the rope was taunt, began to slowly back up.

"It's working; keep going. Slow and steady," Mac called.

Trevor held on to the rope, keeping his feet flat against the rocky cliff. The rope seemed to dig into his body as he slowly climbed upward. Another bolt of lightning directly overhead lit up the sky.

"He's almost to the top," Mac called. "He wants you to hold up."

Trevor climbed up the last few feet and collapsed on the ground near Mac. She dropped to her knees and hugged him tight. "Oh, God, Trev. Are you okay?"

"Yeah, I'm fine. I think I'll have a bruise around my waist from the rope, but I'll be okay as soon as I catch my breath."

Alyson ran up just as the sky opened up, dumping a torrent of rain on the dusty landscape. Mac helped Trevor up and the three of them ran to the safety of the Jeep.

Alyson stopped by Mac and Trevor's houses so they both could change into dry clothing before heading over to hers, where they would test the water and soil samples they had gathered. Alyson changed her own clothes, then started a fire and put on some hot cider while Mac organized her things.

"Got any snacks?" Trevor asked as Alyson poured the cider into blue ceramic mugs.

"You can check the fridge. Mom hasn't cooked much since the carnival started, but I'm sure you can find something."

Trevor rummaged through the refrigerator and cupboards, finally filling a plate with cheese, crackers, slices of apples, and green olives.

"Wow, look at this." Mac was looking through her microscope at a drop of the water Trevor had risked his life to acquire.

"What are we looking at?" Trevor asked as he peered through the small eyepiece.

"The water from the underground river is saturated with toxic chemicals. I can't believe no one has noticed this before. The river must be polluting the ocean big-time. Luckily, the quantity of water that runs into the ocean is pretty small, but still, over time the damage could be catastrophic."

"I wonder where the water's coming from," Alyson murmured. "Someone must be dumping chemicals into the river upstream and it's flowing downstream into the ocean."

"It's going to be hard to figure out where the water originates. It could be anywhere. It's not like we can follow the river upstream; it's under the ground."

"We suspect Chemlab is somehow involved, so I say we start our search there," Alyson concluded.

"Start our search where?" Mac asked.

"At Chemlab. At the plant. We'll need to break in after they close to see if we can find any proof that they're the polluters."

"Breaking into Chemlab isn't going to be like breaking into the town offices," Trevor pointed out. "They'll have security guards and probably an alarm system. Maybe even dogs."

"I didn't say it'd be easy. But really, how else are we going to tie them to the polluted water? We'll need a plan. The best time to break in will be tomorrow night, after everyone leaves for the Christmas holiday. The plant is closed on weekends anyway, and with Christmas being on Monday this year, I'm sure no one will be around until at least Tuesday. We'll go tonight after rehearsal and check things out. If there are dogs and security guards we'll figure out how to get around them."

"What about a security system? How are we going to get around that?" Trevor asked.

"I'm not sure. Maybe if we can get close enough to the building we can figure out what kind of system they have, if they even have one. If we can figure out the kind of system we're dealing with we can call Devon to ask him how to get around it. His dad designs security software for a living; I'm sure he knows how to bypass them."

"I don't know. A large company like Chemlab is bound to have layers of security. I know we've been doing the detective thing lately, but James Bond we're not," Mac insisted.

"Let's just go tonight to see what we find," Alyson pushed. "If the task looks undoable we'll figure something else out. Does anyone know exactly where Chemlab is located?"

"No, but I'll check." Mac's fingers flew over her keyboard. "Oh, hey, they're actually on this side of Portland. Probably not more than a thirty-minute drive. I'll print a map."

"Everyone should wear warm clothes tonight. And bring flashlights," Alyson instructed.

"Yeah, and money for bail. We're probably going to need money for bail." Mac groaned. "Are you sure this is a good idea?"

"It's the only idea," Alyson said. "It'll be fine. It might even be fun. I think I'll wear black. They always wear black in the movies."

It was after nine o'clock by the time rehearsal let out. Alyson, Mackenzie, Trevor, and Tucker all piled into Alyson's Jeep and began the short but seemingly endless drive into the foothills where the plant was located. It was a dark night; the light from the moon was completely blocked by lingering clouds. Alyson switched on the windshield wipers when it started to drizzle.

The steady swish-swish of the wipers as they rotated back and forth was the only sound in the silent vehicle, the occupants lost in their own thoughts. Alyson slowed down as the rain increased, limiting her vision around the tight turns on the curvy road.

"There should be a turn-off on your left in about a mile," Mac said from beside her. "After you turn the plant should be about a half mile up the drive. You might want to kill the headlights once we make the turn, although I have no idea how you'll be able to see anything in the dark. Maybe we should do this on another night, when the moon is out and it's not raining."

"Don't worry; the rain is starting to let up and I can see fine. After I make the turn we'll kill the lights and inch along until we see the plant. I think I see the turn up ahead."

Alyson made the turn and switched off the headlights. She stopped in the road in order to give her eyes time to adjust to the darkness and get her bearings. The rain had slowed to a trickle, vastly improving the visibility.

"Once we see the lights from the plant I'm going to find a place to park and we'll walk from there. All we really want to do tonight is get the lay of the land. Once we know what we're up against we can come up with a plan to actually break in tomorrow night."

Alyson pulled over and parked. Trevor gathered up their flashlights and loaded up his backpack while Alyson put Tucker on the leash.

"I love the smell of rain." Alyson took a deep breath of the fresh air as they started down the road toward the plant.

"We're involved in big-time espionage and you're smelling the air? Aren't you scared at all?" Mac wondered.

"Sure I'm scared, but I'm no less scared if I don't appreciate the rain-fresh air. Trevor's eating a bag of Doritos and you haven't commented on that."

"You're both certifiable. My heart is beating so hard I can barely breathe and you guys are having a snack and sniffing the air."

"Come on, Mac. You hack into computer files all the time and I've never even seen you break a sweat."

"That's different. I'm not worried about someone shooting me, or siccing some big dog on me when I'm involved in computer crime. Maybe I should stick to the white-collar stuff and leave the actual breaking and entering to you two."

"We'll be fine. No actual crimes are being committed here tonight, just a little window-shopping. If you're really uncomfortable you don't have to come along tomorrow. Let's head into the trees so we can look around without being seen."

The large windowless building was constructed from steel and cement. It was completely enclosed by a twenty-foot chain-link fence topped with rows of barbed wire. The large entry gate was opened by a keypad located just outside the gate. There was a single security guard who seemed to make a circular route around the outside of the building.

"Well, at least I don't see any dogs," Mac whispered.

"Yeah, but how are we going to get into the gate?" Trevor asked. "There's no way we're going over the fence."

"I'm not sure," Alyson answered, "The security guard shouldn't be a problem. Once he goes around to the back of the plant we should have at least ten minutes to get through the gate and into the building. I haven't seen him go into the building at all. Every sixty minutes he comes out of the guard building near the front gate and walks around the building. The patrol takes about twenty minutes, then he goes back inside and watches TV until the top of the next hour."

"Even if we figure out a way to get in through the gate, how do we know if we can get into the building? If he's not going inside it must be locked up pretty tight," Trevor pointed out.

"We need to get inside the gate so we can get a look at the security system." Alyson chewed on one of her nails. "If we could figure out the key code one of us could sneak in to check out the building on his next rotation."

"Yeah, but even using a computer program and having an endless amount of time, it'd still be hard to figure out. Out here in the middle of the night sans a computer or time it'd be impossible," Mac said.

"I have an idea." Alyson handed Mac Tucker's leash. "Keep him quiet; I'll be right back"

Alyson pulled her cell phone out of her pocket and started walking down the paved road toward the entry gate and the unsuspecting security guard.

"Excuse me," Alyson addressed the man as he came out of the guard shack when she walked up. "My car broke down and I've been trying to call my father, but my cell phone isn't getting service out here." She held up her cell phone and pointed it toward the guard. "Do you think I could use your phone?"

"Sure, I've got one in here. Hang on; I'll get the gate."

The guard walked over to the keypad, which was on his side of the gate, and punched in a series of numbers while Alyson continued to hold up her phone, as if she was searching for those elusive lines. The gate swung open and Alyson put her cell phone in her pocket and followed the guard into the small building.

"I really appreciate your help." Alyson picked up the phone and pretended to dial. "Hi, Daddy. Sorry to wake you, but my car broke down. Can you come get me?" She paused, as if she was listening to his response. "I know, I'm sorry. I'm not sure; hang on." Alyson turned toward the guard. "I need to tell my father how to find me. My car is just down the road; do you happen to know what the name of the road is?"

"Old Timber Road."

"Thanks."

"Daddy, I'm about twenty miles up Old Timber Road. My car is just off to the side of the road. I'm not sure if it's just out of gas or if it's something more. Okay, I'll wait in the car."

Alyson hung up and returned to the gate, where the guard was now waiting. "Thanks, I really appreciate this. My dad should be here soon."

"What's a pretty young thing doing out here all alone in the middle of the night anyway?"

"I'm afraid I took a wrong turn, then got lost. My car quit running just down the road. I might be out of gas, but the things been real temperamental lately, so I'm not sure. Thanks again for your help."

"I'd give you a ride into town myself but I'd catch hell if I left my post even for a short while. If I don't do a security patrol every hour on the hour my boss comes unglued."

"Really? How does he even know if you do your patrols or not? It's not like anyone else is around to tell on you if you miss one."

"There are security cameras on the exterior of the premises. He watches the tapes sometimes to check up on me."

"Oh, I see. Well, I hope you don't get into trouble for helping me out tonight."

"Actually, the only cameras that even work anymore are around back. I keep telling the administration that they need to upgrade their security. They have an almost obsolete system for such a large facility. I don't think they've done a single upgrade in twenty years."

"It seems like you know a lot about these things. What would you do differently if it were up to you?"

"Don't even get me started. The building itself has an old Titan system. I don't think they even make those anymore. A kindergartener could break into this place. First thing I'd do is install a Centrex 2500. Now *that's* a security system. Not only is there an alarm, but if there's an unauthorized entry into the building there are heat sensors and motion detectors inside. With the old system they have now you're pretty much home free if you can get in the door without setting off the alarm."

"Why do you think the company hasn't taken your advice to upgrade? It seems like you have some pretty good ideas."

"I guess they figure no one would want to break in here anyway. It's not like there's a lot of valuable stuff inside. The second floor is just offices and stuff. Nothing of value there. I don't even think they've upgraded their computers in quite a while. The equipment downstairs is way too heavy for someone to just walk off with."

"Maybe they can't afford to upgrade the system. I'll bet it's pretty pricey."

"Money's not a problem. They paved this whole lot last year. Almost forty acres. Now you know that amount of concrete had to have cost a fortune."

"The lot wasn't always paved?"

"No. It was just dirt until early last year. Don't know why they did it. It doesn't really seem to make much of a difference. Why go to all the trouble and expense of covering up dirt with concrete when all you're going to do is park on it? I guess it could have been because of the mud."

"Mud?"

"Yeah, the drainage in the area is the worst. Sometimes we'd have standing water for weeks after a good rain."

Alyson looked at her watch. "Well, I'd better get going. My dad should be here soon. Besides, you need to start your patrol. Thanks again for all your help."

"No problem. I hope everything works out okay with the car."

Alyson smiled and waved at the man as she walked back toward the spot where her friends were waiting.

"My God, Alyson." Mac grabbed her arm and pulled her over to where she and Trevor were hiding.

"Are you crazy? What'd you say? What'd he say? You had this whole conversation with the guy. Did you just saunter up and ask him for the key code? Are you nuts?"

"If you want to know, you might let her get a word in edgewise," Trevor said with a nervous laugh.

"Let's go back to the car," Alyson suggested. "I'll fill you in on the way home."

Alyson headed back the way they'd come. Once she reached the main road she turned on the headlights and picked up speed. The rain had stopped completely, but the roads were still damp, making driving cautiously a must on the narrow, winding road.

"So," Mac asked impatiently, "what gives? Did you get the key code?"

Alyson handed Mac her phone. "Go into the photo file and check out the five newest pictures."

Mac did as instructed. "Alyson, you're a genius. I totally renounce my own title as group genius and turn it over to you."

"What?" Trevor asked from the backseat.

"Alyson managed to take a sequence of photos on her camera showing the security guard opening the gate for her. The key code is 5-7-9-3."

"I thought you said there were five photos."

"I was just shooting continuous shots. I guess I shot one more than necessary."

"Didn't the guard think it was strange that you were taking his picture as he opened the gate?" Trevor asked.

"He didn't know. I told him my car broke down and I couldn't get any reception on my cell. I asked him if I could use his phone to call my dad. While he punched in the code I held the phone up, like I was still looking for bars. Poor guy never suspected a thing."

"Wow, I think I have to agree with Mac. You *are* a genius. But if we got the code why didn't we stay to try to check out the security system?"

"Didn't need to. Thanks to the talkative guard, I managed to find out that the only system is an antiquated Titan. That means nothing to me, but I'm sure it will to Devon. The guard also told me that although the plant has external security cameras, only the ones in the back work, so if we stay to the front of the building we should be able to get in undetected. Once we're in the building there are no further security measures."

"It's beginning to sound like we might almost be able to pull this off. If college doesn't work out as planned, you could always have a career as a master thief," Trevor complimented her.

"Thanks, but I think I'll limit my breaking and entering to helping out the good guys."

Chapter 14

By the time they'd gotten back to Cutter's Cove the previous night it was almost morning, so they decided to meet to discuss their plan for the evening the next day at lunch. After placing their orders, Alyson filled Mac and Trevor in on her conversation with Devon.

"He said bypassing the Titan system would be a cinch. I'm going to call him when we get to the plant tonight and he'll walk us through it. We need to bring a few basic tools—a screwdriver, wire cutters, a small wrench. He also said to bring your laptop, just in case."

"I really miss Eli. I hope they're having fun. Did he say if they were having fun?"

"It sounded like fun was being had."

"Okay, so we use the key code Alyson got last night to get in through the gate," Trevor began to summarize, "then we call Devon once we get inside the yard and he tells us how to get past the security system and into the building. Then what?"

"We look around. The offices are on the second floor. I suggest we start there. The guard does his walk-around on the hour, so we'll just have to time our escape to coincide with the time he's around the back side of the building."

"What exactly are we looking for?" Trevor asked.

"I'm not sure. Anything that will link Chemlab to Mrs. Conway's kidnapping, the missing mayor, or the sabotage at the carnival would be helpful, but what we really need is a link to the toxic waste we found in the water."

"Okay. Scenario," Mac began. "What if the key code changes each day or the guard varies his routine?"

"I thought of that, but the guard said the security system was antiquated and hadn't been updated in years. I'm betting they don't bother to change the key code if they don't fix the video monitors in the front of the building. As for the guard's routine, he indicated that the owner was a stickler for timeliness, so I doubt that will be a problem."

"I'll bring the tools," Trevor offered. "What else do we need?"

"That's all I can think of. The town spaghetti dinner is tonight and we're all scheduled to help out, so we won't be able to head out until after we finish cleaning up, around nine. We'll all need to bring warm, dark-colored clothes to change into."

"So what now?" Mac asked. "We have several hours before we need to be in the auditorium for hair and makeup for dress rehearsal."

"I think it's best to stay busy. Maybe we should go find our moms to see if they need any help," Alyson said.

The scene that greeted them when they got downtown was complete mayhem. There were police cars everywhere and people were standing around as if in a daze.

"What's going on?" Alyson asked the first person she came across.

"Didn't you hear? They found the mayor floating facedown in the ocean."

"What?" Alyson was stunned.

"Some fishermen came across him first thing this morning. The police have been here all morning, going through his files and questioning pretty much everyone."

"How awful." Alyson glanced at Mac and Trevor. "Does anyone know what happened? How he died?"

"I'm not sure. The police aren't saying much at this point. I guess he must have drowned. I mean, he was floating in the ocean."

"Yeah, probably. Thanks."

Alyson, Mac, and Trevor wandered off away from the crowd.

"First Mrs. Conway and now the mayor." Mac groaned. "Who would do such a thing?"

"It's got to be linked to Chemlab," Alyson postulated.

"But I thought we assumed the mayor was working with someone from Chemlab. Why would they kill him?"

"He must have become more of a liability than a help. I wonder how we can find out more about what's going on."

"Chelsea," Trevor suggested. "She seems to be in the know. I'll give her a call."

Trevor spoke with her for a few minutes and hung up his cell phone. "The mayor was definitely murdered. He was shot before he was dumped in the ocean. The police are speculating that he was probably killed sometime last night. The fish have been nibbling on the body, though, so it's a little hard to tell without running tests."

"Ew. You mean he's all eaten up?" Alyson asked.

"Pretty much."

"If he was killed last night he's been alive this whole time. He's been missing for a week. I wonder why they killed him now," Mac said. "What changed in the past twenty-four hours?"

"I hate to say it, but it seems like things intensified after we requested the canceled check. We might be responsible for his death," Alyson guessed.

"We also found Mrs. Conway," Trevor reminded her. "Her being found alive and talking might have been a trigger."

"Either way, it looks like our actions might have been the catalyst that turned the tables on the mayor," Alyson commented. "I wanted him to go to prison for what he did, not die."

"Our actions might have backed the bad guys into a corner where the mayor was concerned," Mac said, "but at least we saved Mrs. Conway. She was the innocent victim here. Whatever happened to the mayor, he brought it on himself."

"Chelsea also told me they're considering canceling the carnival and the play. They're going to have an emergency town council meeting to decide. In fact," Trevor looked at his watch, "they should be meeting right now."

"As much as I'd welcome an excuse not to have to parade around in front of the whole town in my skimpy Christmas Present outfit, I hope they don't cancel the whole thing. The town still needs the money and everyone's worked really hard rehearsing all week."

"Chelsea said she'd call when she found out more."

"If the council is going to cancel the play they'll have to decide soon. I think the preparations are already underway for the spaghetti dinner. Let's find our moms to see if they've heard anything," Mac suggested. "I bet mine is over in the auditorium."

"Good idea." Alyson walked between Mac and Trevor toward the large brick building.

As it turned out, not only was Mac's mom in the kitchen, helping to prepare the evening's meal, but Alyson and Trevor's moms were there too.

"Did you hear what happened?" Sarah said as she came into the room.

They nodded.

"This town used to be such a nice, peaceful place." Mac's mom shook her head. "I don't know what the world is coming to when a friendly town like Cutter's Cove has so many tragedies in one week. First the body that was found in the cemetery, then poor Mrs. Conway's abduction, and now the mayor. Whatever is going on?"

"Did you hear anything else? About the mayor, I mean. Like how he died or who they think might be responsible?" Mac asked her.

"No, the police are keeping it quiet. I just don't know who would do such a thing to such a perfectly nice man. Mayor Gregor was just the kindest, most caring person. The whole thing makes no sense. And now there's talk of canceling the carnival and dinner tonight. What am I supposed to do with all this food? We planned to serve three hundred and fifty dinners. Who's going to eat all this?"

"I'm sure the town council will take all that into account," Mac comforted her mom.

"I spoke to Rochelle Green, and she said her husband planned to suggest that they continue with tonight's plans in spite of the tragedy," Trevor's mom added. "Dr. Went is out of town and the Whites have already left for the Bahamas, so it's just George Green, Elsa Forrester, and Mike Jordan who are meeting. In fact, the Greens are supposed to leave in the morning for St. Croix, but Rochelle said their plans are up in the air now, with everything that's happened."

"Chelsea's got to love that," Mac mumbled under her breath.

"I think the best thing to do at this point is to proceed as if nothing has changed," Sarah suggested. "We have a lot of lettuce to chop and bread to butter if we hope to be ready to start serving by five."

"Can we help?" Alyson asked.

"Pull up a knife. The more the merrier."

The town council voted unanimously not to cancel the play, and the spaghetti dinner was a huge success. There was a momentary panic when it looked like they might run short of food, but Alyson suggested decreasing the portions served to young children, who never finished anyway, thereby increasing the total number of dinners that could be served. By the time the kitchen was cleaned and the auditorium set to rights for the Christmas play the next evening, everyone was completely exhausted.

"Are you sure we need to break into Chemlab tonight?" Mac asked. "Because right now I'm thinking a long winter's nap is much more appealing. I don't think I can feel my feet after standing in one place serving spaghetti for three hours."

"It has to be tonight. Tomorrow we have the play, Sunday is Christmas Eve, Monday is Christmas, and Tuesday we leave for Canada. It's now or never," Alyson reminded her.

"And I suppose never isn't really an option?"

"Come on, Mac, we'll stop for coffee on the way," Trevor offered. "Do you have your laptop?"

"It's in my car. I'll get it."

Once they were on the road tension woke everyone up. The only one sleeping peacefully was Tucker, who was stretched out in the cargo area behind the backseat. Alyson had turned the radio on low and "Jolly Old Saint Nicholas" was playing in the background.

"I can't believe Christmas is in three days." Mac sighed. "I haven't even finished my shopping. One way or the other, I have to go tomorrow or my sisters won't be getting any gifts from me. I bought Kyle a video game, and I got my dad a new fishing pole and my mom a really great sweater. I still have no idea what to get for Eli. Any suggestions?"

"I'm not the one to ask, and I haven't even started my shopping yet," Alyson answered. "But I'm up for going with you tomorrow. How about you, Trev? Want to come?"

"Yeah, I'll come, but I'm totally finished with my shopping. I get everyone on my list a gift certificate for Bergman's Department Store every year. I don't even have to wrap them; they come in nice little envelopes."

"That doesn't seem very imaginative or personal," Alyson said.

"It's what I do. I'm the gift card guy and everyone knows it."

"Actually, I kind of like those gift cards," Mac commented. "I can get what I want and I don't have to worry about taking anything back."

"You guys exchange presents?" Alyson asked.

"Yeah, ever since the first grade, when I wrapped up my prize marble and gave it to Trev. Last year I got him this really exotic-looking sweater that he never wears."

"I wear it. In the dark. Under a coat."

Mac glared at him.

"Oh, come on, Mac, it's got green, yellow, and orange stripes."

"Okay, it wasn't my best gift idea. But hey, the year before I got you those cool sunglasses. You seemed to really like those."

"I did. Nice and plain and black. I could use another pair, if you're looking for gift ideas."

"No, I already know what I'm getting you, and it isn't sunglasses or a crazy sweater. I think you'll really like it."

"How about a hint?"

"Sorry, you'll have to wait until Christmas Eve, when we always exchange gifts. Trevor and I usually do breakfast or lunch together before all the family stuff starts. Can you join us this year? I wasn't sure what your plans were."

"Yeah, it sounds like fun," Alyson said. "Just let me know when and where. I think we're almost to the turn-off. It's really dark again tonight; help me look."

"I think that's it just ahead." Mac pointed in the distance.

After Alyson had parked off to the side they went over their plans one last time. Once inside, Alyson would call Devon, while Trevor followed his instructions. They figured they had ten minutes at the most from the time the guard went around the corner of the building until he emerged on the other side.

"We should have timed this better," Mac realized. "It's twenty minutes until the top of the hour. A person could go crazy with twenty minutes of waiting."

"So, do you think Eli's hooked up with any snow bunnies this week?" Trevor asked to distract her.

"I'm sure he hasn't. He's not you. His attention span is longer than ten minutes. I sure do miss him, though."

"Hey, why don't we call Devon early?" Alyson suggested. "It'd be best to already have him on the line before the clock starts, and if he's around you can talk to Eli in the meantime."

"Are you sure? I wouldn't want to run up your bill."

"That's okay. I have unlimited calling."

Alyson dialed Devon's number and waited while it rang. "Hi, Dev. We're here. Yeah, I've got everything. Listen, is Eli there? We have a few minutes before the guard leaves on his rounds and Mac wanted to say hi."

Alyson handed Mac the phone. "You have ten minutes. Trevor and I will be outside, checking out the situation."

"We will?" Trevor asked. "It's cold out there."

"Come on, stud. Let's give Mac some privacy. Besides, we really should get the lay of the land."

Alyson buttoned up her coat and put Tucker on the leash, then they quietly snuck around to the front of the fence so she could see into the guardhouse.

"Good; it's the same guard who was here last night. I didn't have the impression he'd shoot us even if he did happen to catch us in the act. He was actually a pretty nice guy. It must be lonely out here, all by himself at night."

"People who hang out alone in the dark usually have a reason. Maybe he likes the quiet, or maybe he doesn't like people," Trevor said.

"Could be."

Mac joined them several minutes later and handed Alyson her phone. "Thanks. Devon wants to talk to you before we go in."

"Hey, Dev. What's up?"

"Are you sure you want to do this? Mac told Eli about the mayor. You've already rescued Mrs. Conway, and with the mayor's death, it really doesn't seem like there's much urgency anymore. Maybe you should just turn everything you've found over to the police and let them sort it out. Why risk jail time or worse when no lives are in danger?" Devon asked her.

"Yeah, I guess. I just hate to quit before we finish."

"You know if you break in and don't find anything you're going to get the security guard fired. The only way to bypass the system without more technical equipment than you have is to cut the wires. By the time they open on Tuesday, Chemlab will know they've been broken into even if you do manage to get in and out without setting off the alarm."

"Someone's coming up the road," Mac whispered urgently behind her. "We'd better get out of sight."

"Hang on, Dev," Alyson said into the phone. "Someone's coming."

They snuck around into the cover of the trees that lined the road. Alyson had been careful to park the

Jeep out of sight, so she didn't think that'd be a problem. "Tucker, quiet," Alyson commanded as he growled at the passing truck. A large black truck.

"Mac, take Tucker back to the Jeep. I want to get a better look at the guy in the truck, but I don't want to risk Tucker barking and giving us away."

"I'll come with you," Trevor whispered to Alyson.

Trevor and Alyson slowly started walking toward the fence, where they could get a better look at the truck. There was no moon, which made sneaking through the trees undetected easier.

"Doesn't he look like the guy from the photo?" Alyson breathed. "The plant foreman. The one the mayor was arguing with and the bookkeeper was having lunch with?"

"Yeah, and he's tall too. He could fit the description Mrs. Conway gave us of the man who attacked her."

"What are you kids doing here?" a voice demanded from behind, just before Alyson felt the barrel of a gun in her back.

"Mrs. Cranston?" Alyson gasped.

"I had a feeling it was you kids who've been snooping around all week. You were lucky sneaking into my office without getting caught, but it looks like your luck has just run out. Where's the other one? The redhead?"

"She didn't come with us tonight. She's home sick with a cold," Alyson lied.

"Well, you two are about to wish you had stayed home with your little friend. Now start walking. Carl's going to be real interested in talking to you."

"I don't get it. Why are you involved in this?" Alyson asked as they walked. "The mayor? Mrs. Conway? These are people you've worked with for years. How could you be involved in hurting them?"

"That stupid mayor actually thought he could embezzle money and I wouldn't find out. I was having an affair with him for two years until he left me for that whore Rita Farrell. I knew him better than he knew himself. Of course I would notice the phony checks. I mean, he named the company after himself and endorsed the checks himself. The man was a complete idiot. He deserved to die."

"And Mrs. Conway? Did she deserve to die? Because she almost did."

"No, that was unfortunate. If that dope Dr. Went hadn't left the folder with the financial stuff in it with her, she wouldn't have been involved at all. I have to say I was glad to hear that you kids found her in time, although her rescue did complicate things a bit. Carl might have to kill her after all."

"It's not too late. You can let us go," Trevor reasoned. "So far you haven't actually killed anyone. Unless you were the one who shot the mayor."

"No, Carl had the pleasure, but given the chance I would have done it in a minute. Now get inside." She indicated the open door that Carl and the security guard had walked through minutes earlier. Pulling the door closed behind her, she made sure the alarm was set before she shoved Alyson down the darkened hallway, causing her to trip over what could only be the body of the guard.

Trevor grabbed her arm and steadied her. "Do you have your cell phone?" he whispered.

"No, I dropped it when she startled us. Dev was still on the line, though. Hopefully, he heard what happened and called the police."

"What are you two whispering about?"

"Nothing," Alyson replied. "We were just wondering who I tripped over and if he was alive."

"That stupid guard. I have no idea if Carl killed him or simply knocked him out. Doesn't matter. You'll all be dead within the hour. Now get in that office and sit down."

Mrs. Cranston shoved Alyson and Trevor into two aluminum chairs arranged in front of the desk.

"What do we have here?" Carl asked.

"These are the kids who have been causing all the trouble. I found them lurking outside. They know too much, I think they were responsible for breaking into my office and ordering the check from the bank."

"I see. Shouldn't you kids be hanging out at the mall instead of messing in stuff that's none of your business? Now I'm going to have two more bodies to dispose of. You have no idea what a pain in the ass that is."

"I'm sorry to inconvenience you, but you could make it easier on all of us and let us go," Alyson suggested.

"And why would I do that?"

Alyson reached for an answer. "Because it's Christmas. And you don't want to have to deal with the discomfort and inconvenience of a guilty conscious."

"Oh, my conscious will be fine."

Alyson looked toward the door and nodded her head ever so slightly.

"Why'd you do it? Why'd you hook up with the mayor and start this whole thing in the first place?" Alyson asked. "The phony company, the sabotage of the carnival, the murder of the grad student?"

"You figured out all that, did you?" Carl asked.

"That and more. I just don't get why. Why risk your company, your reputation, your very life and freedom to buy some old cemetery?"

"You think I'd tell you?"

"What difference does it make? You're going to kill us anyway. Who are we going to tell?"

"True. Oh, hell, why not?" Carl shrugged. "You've gone to all the trouble of figuring this much out. Turns out there's an underground stream beneath this property that runs all the way to the ocean. Some nosy grad student figured out that the chemical pollution in the area actually originated here. Seems we had a few unreported chemical spills over the years. Anyway, I thought I had taken care of the evidence by paving the whole bloody lot; then that nosy Goody Two-Shoes came around asking questions. I had no choice but to kill him. I decided the best way to cover up the evidence he uncovered was to buy the land and pave over that too. Didn't know it'd be such a hassle. I mean, really, who cares about a bunch of old graves? I bribed the mayor to push the sale through and thought that would be the end of it. Would have been too, if you kids hadn't gotten involved."

"We read that you were investigated for chemical waste violations last year. Who ratted you out in the first place?" Alyson asked.

"Boy, you kids really did do your homework, didn't you? If you must know, one of my former employees—a *deceased* former employee—decided it was his civic duty to report our little accidents to the authorities. Luckily, I managed to persuade the man to tell me everything he had reported and realized that paving the complex would solve my little problem. Cost me a pretty penny too."

"What about Ian Wall, the owner of Chemlab? How does he fit into all this?"

"He doesn't. Mr. Wall passed away last year, just before the investigation began."

"You killed him."

"Had to. He hadn't known about the spills. He wanted to cooperate with the authorities. Stupid man. I'm forever surrounded by stupid men who end up getting themselves killed."

"But how can he be dead?" Alyson asked. "He just signed papers to incorporate Psycorp a few months ago. And I saw a newspaper article that said he was involved in the investigation of Chemlab last year."

"Interesting thing about old Ian; he had a twin brother who was more than willing to sign a few documents and take a few pictures."

"He was involved in killing his own brother?" Alyson grimaced.

"No, I told him Ian died in an accident, but if he reported it his estate and all his millions would be tied up in probate for the rest of his life. Better to pretend to be him on a few select occasions and save the hassle. As far as the rest of the world knows, Ian is alive and well, just out of the country."

"Just shoot them already," Mrs. Cranston said from behind him.

"With pleasure." Carl held up the gun and aimed it at Alyson's head.

"Now!" Alyson yelled.

"What the...?" Carl screamed as Tucker attacked him from behind and clamped onto his neck. He fell to the floor and dropped the gun, which skidded across the floor. Mac ran forward and picked it up, pointing it at a stunned bookkeeper and a screaming plant foreman.

"Tucker, come," Alyson demanded.

Tucker let go of the bleeding man's neck but continued to growl.

"Devon overheard Mrs. Cranston coming up behind you," Mac said as she shakily held the gun on the pair. "He called the police. They should be here any minute."

"Way to go, Mac." Trevor took the gun from Mac's shaking hand. "How'd you get in? I saw Mrs. Cranston set the alarm."

"Alyson dropped her phone along the way. I picked it up and Devon was still on the line. He talked me through the process. Piece of cake. Really." She started to fall as her shaky legs gave way. Trevor grabbed her with his free hand and steadied her.

"I saw you with the phone in your hand." Alyson carefully snuck around behind and went to stand by her friends, putting her arm around Mac's waist in support. "I was hoping Devon was still on the line."

"He recorded the whole thing. I think, Mr. Reinhart, you've provided the police with a very thorough confession."

"You damn kids." He started to lunge toward them until Tucker's very unfriendly bark stopped him.

"I hear the sirens now. I'll go open the door so they can get in, although the security system is quite dead," Mac said.

Chapter 15

"I'm so glad it's finally over," Alyson said two days later as she and her friends gathered to share a Christmas Eve brunch.

"I know what you mean." Mac took a sip of her hot cider. "I've never been so scared in my life. I thought I would die. I'll be having nightmares for weeks."

"It wasn't so bad." Trevor buttered one of the warm croissants the waitress had just set down on the table.

"Maybe not for you," Mac countered. "I thought I was prepared. I really did. But when I looked out at the two hundred or so people in the audience last night I totally froze. I'm good at stuff. I'm not used to being so totally inept. I can't believe I couldn't remember any of my lines."

"No one even noticed," Alyson lied. "Gordy Collins totally covered for you."

"You think so?" Mac asked hopefully.

"I know so."

"Well, I'll tell you one thing: next year I'm sticking to painting backdrops," Mac decided. "I'm not cut out to be in the spotlight."

"I didn't think I was either," Alyson said, "but it turns out I had a lot of fun."

"This omelet is excellent." Trevor cut off a large bite. "How are your eggs Benedict?" he asked Mac.

"Really good. The ham is fresh sliced, not that processed stuff. And the hollandaise sauce is to die for."

"I can't believe it's Christmas Eve already." Alyson took a bite of her own veggie scramble. "I really enjoyed the carnival, but I'm glad it's over. I may have to sleep through Christmas Day to be rested enough to make the trip on Tuesday."

"I wish I could sleep through the day, but my aunts and uncles and all my cousins are coming over this afternoon and it'll be nonstop holiday merriment until they leave tomorrow night." Mac spread some fresh raspberry jelly on her roll. "At least I finally finished my shopping. I can't tell you what a relief that is."

"What'd you decide to get for Eli? I went with a cashmere sweater for Devon. Nice but noncommittal."

"I made a collage of the two of us. Pictures from the beach and the bonfire and the football games. Stuff like that. I know, it's dorky, but I couldn't think of anything that said 'hey, I care about you, but I'm not ready to jump into bed with you.' I'm sure he'll hate it."

"He'll love it. It's thoughtful and personal. Seriously, it's perfect. Don't you think, Trev?"

"Sure, why not? So what'd you get for me? I noticed you brought some packages in with you. Here's my gift card. I even put a bow on it."

"After we finish eating. I want to keep the suspense alive as long as possible."

"I'm done." He put down his fork even thought his plate was half full.

"Well, I'm not. This whole holiday season has sped by in a blur. I want to take a moment to savor this time I have alone with my two best friends.

Canada will be fun and I miss Eli a lot, but I like it when it's just us."

"To us." Alyson held up her orange juice glass. "Best friends forever."

Books by Kathi Daley

Come for the murder, stay for the romance.
Buy them on Amazon today.

Zoe Donovan Cozy Mystery:

Halloween Hijinks
The Trouble With Turkeys
Christmas Crazy
Cupid's Curse
Big Bunny Bump-off
Beach Blanket Barbie
Maui Madness
Derby Divas
Haunted Hamlet
Turkeys, Tuxes, and Tabbies
Christmas Cozy
Alaskan Alliance
Matrimony Meltdown
Soul Surrender
Heavenly Honeymoon
Hopscotch Homicide
Ghostly Graveyard
Santa Sleuth – *December 2015*

Paradise Lake Cozy Mystery:

Pumpkins in Paradise
Snowmen in Paradise
Bikinis in Paradise
Christmas in Paradise
Puppies in Paradise
Halloween in Paradise

Whales and Tails Cozy Mystery:

Romeow and Juliet
The Mad Catter
Grimm's Furry Tail
Much Ado About Felines
The Legend of Tabby Hollow
Cat of Christmas Past – *November 2015*

Seacliff High Mystery:

The Secret
The Curse
The Relic
The Conspiracy
The Grudge – *December 2015*

Road to Christmas Romance:

Road to Christmas Past

Kathi Daley lives with her husband, kids, grandkids, and Bernese mountain dogs in beautiful Lake Tahoe. When she isn't writing, she likes to read (preferably at the beach or by the fire), cook (preferably something with chocolate or cheese), and garden (planting and planning, not weeding). She also enjoys spending time on the water when she's not hiking, biking, or snowshoeing the miles of desolate trails surrounding her home.

Kathi uses the mountain setting in which she lives, along with the animals (wild and domestic) that share her home, as inspiration for her cozy mysteries.

Stay up-to-date with her newsletter, *The Daley Weekly*. There's a link to sign up on both her Facebook page and her website, or you can access the sign-in sheet at: http://eepurl.com/NRPDf

Visit Kathi:
Facebook at Kathi Daley Books,
www.facebook.com/kathidaleybooks

Kathi Daley Teen –
www.facebook.com/kathidaleyteen

Kathi Daley Books Group Page –
https://www.facebook.com/groups/5695788231468
50/

Kathi Daley Books Birthday Club- get a book on your birthday -

https://www.facebook.com/groups/1040638412628912/

Kathi Daley Recipe Exchange - https://www.facebook.com/groups/752806778126428/

Webpage - www.kathidaley.com

E-mail - kathidaley@kathidaley.com

Recipe Submission E-mail – kathidaleyrecipes@kathidaley.com

Goodreads: https://www.goodreads.com/author/show/7278377.Kathi_Daley

Twitter at Kathi Daley@kathidaley - https://twitter.com/kathidaley

Tumblr - http://kathidaleybooks.tumblr.com/

Amazon Author Page - http://www.amazon.com/author/kathidaley

Pinterest - http://www.pinterest.com/kathidaley/

24753651R00114

Made in the USA
San Bernardino, CA
06 October 2015